"Sorry, I didn't mean to take advantage of you like that," he told her, still cupping her cheek with the palm of his hand.

Her voice felt as if it was going to crack at any second as she told him, "You didn't. And there's nothing to be sorry about, except..."

"Except?" he prodded.

Lily shook her head, not wanting to continue. She was only going to embarrass herself—and him—if she said anything further. "I've said too much."

"No," he contradicted, "you've said too little. "'Except' what?" he coaxed.

Lily wavered. Maybe he did deserve to know. So she told him.

"Except maybe it didn't last long enough," she said, her voice hardly above a whisper, her cheeks burning and threatening to turn a deep pink.

"Maybe it didn't," he agreed. "Let's see if I get it right this time," he murmured just before his mouth came down on hers for a second time.

* * *

MATCHMAKING MAMAS:
Playing Cupid. Arranging dates. What are mothers for?

Dear Reader,

This Matchmaking Mamas story deals with a topic near and dear to my heart: pets. I got my very first pet in my late thirties, a German shepherd named Rocky. I had always wanted a pet, but my family had been too poor while I was growing up. This four-legged creature running around the house was a new experience.

When Rocky's time came to leave us, I couldn't stand the void. After a short grieving period, we adopted "Audrey Hepburn" from the local German Shepherd Rescue Society. Audrey came to live with us on December 6 (which, if you're Polish—or Dutch—is also known as Santa Claus Day) and changed our lives.

Jonathan, the Labrador puppy in the story, is a melded form of Rocky and Audrey—and how they were trained—and trained me. Oh, yes, and two remarkable people are brought together by the dog. Hope you like them.

As always, I thank you for reading, and from the bottom of my heart, I wish you someone to love who loves you back.

All my best,

Marie

Diamond in the Ruff

Marie Ferrarella

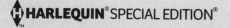
HARLEQUIN®SPECIAL EDITION®

Recycling programs
for this product may
not exist in your area.

ISBN-13: 978-0-373-65844-2

DIAMOND IN THE RUFF

Copyright © 2014 by Marie Rydzynski-Ferrarella

Printed in U.S.A.

MARIE FERRARELLA

This *USA TODAY* bestselling and RITA® Award-winning author has written more than two hundred books for Harlequin, some under the name Marie Nicole. Her romances are beloved by fans worldwide. Visit her website, www.marieferrarella.com.

To
Rocky and Audrey
who made my life so much richer
in their own unique way.

Prologue

"You don't remember me, do you?"

Maizie Connors, youthful grandmother, successful Realtor and matchmaker par excellence, looked at the tall, handsome, blond-haired young man standing in the doorway of her real estate office. Mentally, she whizzed through the many faces she had encountered in the past handful of years, both professionally and privately. Try as she might to recall the young man, Maizie came up empty. His smile was familiar, but the rest of him was not.

Ever truthful, Maizie made no attempt to bluff her way through this encounter until she either remembered him or, more to the point, the young man said something that would set off flares in her somewhat overtaxed brain, reminding her who he was.

Instead, Maizie shook her head and admitted, "I'm afraid I don't."

"I was a lot younger back then and I guess I looked more like a blond swizzle stick than anything else," he told her.

She didn't remember the face, but the smile and now the voice nudged at something distant within her mind. Recognition was still frustratingly out of reach. The young man's voice was lower, but the cadence was very familiar. She'd heard it before.

"Your voice is familiar and that smile, I know I've seen it before, but…" Maizie's voice trailed off as she continued to study his face. "I know I didn't sell you a house," she told him with certainty. She would have remembered that.

She remembered *all* of her clients as well as all the couples she, Theresa and Cecilia had brought together over the past few years. As far as Maizie was concerned, she and her lifelong best friends had all found their true calling in life a few years ago when desperation to see their single children married and on their way to creating their own families had the women using their connections in the three separate businesses they owned to find suitable matches for their offspring.

Enormously successful in their undertaking, they found they couldn't stop just because they had run out of their own children to work with. So friends and clients were taken on.

They did their best work covertly, not allowing the two principals in the undertaking know that they were being paired up. The payment the three exacted was not monetary. It was the deep satisfaction that came from knowing they had successfully brought two soul mates together.

But the young man before her was neither a professional client nor a private one. Yet he *was* familiar.

Shrugging her shoulders in a gesture of complete surrender, Maizie said, "I'm afraid you're going to have to take pity on me and tell me why your smile and your voice are so familiar but the rest of you isn't." Even as she said the words aloud, a partial answer suddenly occurred to her. "You're someone's son, aren't you?"

But whose? she wondered. She hadn't been at either of her "careers"—neither the one involving real estate nor the one aimed at finding soul mates—long enough for this young man to have been the result of her work.

So who are you?

"I was," he told her, his blue eyes on hers.

Was.

The moment he said that, it suddenly came to her. "You're Frances Whitman's boy, aren't you?"

He grinned. "Mom always said you were exceedingly sharp. Yes, I'm Frances's son." He said the words with pride.

The name instantly conjured up an image in Maizie's mind, the image of a woman with laughing blue eyes and an easy smile on her lips—always, no matter what adversity she was valiantly facing.

The same smile she was looking at right now.

"Christopher?" Maizie asked haltingly. "Christopher Whitman!" It was no longer a question but an assertion. Maizie threw her arms around him, giving him a warm, fond embrace, which only reached as far up as his chest. "How *are* you?" she asked with enthusiasm.

"I'm doing well, thanks." And then he told her why he'd popped in after all this time. "And it looks like we're going to be neighbors."

"Neighbors?" Maizie repeated, somewhat confused.

There'd been no For Sale signs up on her block. Infinitely aware of every house that went up for sale not just in her neighborhood, but in her city as well, Maizie knew her friend's son was either mistaken or had something confused.

"Yes, I just rented out the empty office two doors down from you," he told her, referring to the strip mall where her real estate office was located.

"Rented it out?" she repeated, waiting for him to tell her just what line of work he was in without having to specifically ask him.

Christopher nodded. "Yes, I thought this was a perfect location for my practice."

She raised her eyebrows in minor surprise and admiration.

"You're a doctor?" It was the first thing she thought of since her own daughter was a pediatrician.

Christopher nodded. "Of furry creatures, large and small," he annotated.

"You're a vet," she concluded.

"—erinarian," he amended. "I find if I just say I'm a vet, I have people thanking me for my service to this country. I don't want to mislead anyone," he explained with a smile she now found dazzling.

"Either way, you'll have people thanking you," Maizie assured him. She took a step back to get a better, fuller view of the young man. He had certainly filled out since she had seen him last. "Christopher Whitman," she repeated in amazement. "You look a great deal like your mother."

"I'll take that as a compliment," he said with a warm smile. "I was always grateful that you and the other ladies were there for Mom while she was getting her treatments. She didn't tell me she was sick until it was close to the end," he explained. It was a sore point for him, but under the circumstances, he'd had to forgive his mother. There hadn't been any time left for wounded feelings. "You know how she was. Very proud."

"Of you," Maizie emphasized. "I remember her telling me that she didn't want to interfere with your schooling. She knew you'd drop out if you thought she needed you."

"I would have," he answered without hesitation.

She heard the note of sadness in his voice that time still hadn't managed to erase. Maizie quickly changed the subject. Frances wouldn't have wanted her son to beat himself up over a decision she had made for him.

"A veterinarian, huh? So what else is new since I last saw you?" Maizie asked.

Broad shoulders rose and fell in a careless shrug. "Nothing much."

Habit had Maizie glancing down at his left hand. It was bare, but that didn't necessarily mean the man wasn't married. "No Mrs. Veterinarian?"

Christopher laughed softly and shook his head. "Haven't had the time to find the right woman," he confessed. It wasn't the truth, but he had no desire to revisit that painful area yet. "I know Mom would have hated to hear that excuse, but that's just the way things are. Well, when I saw your name on the door, I just wanted to drop by to say hi," he told her, adding, "Stop by the office sometime when you get a chance and we'll talk some more about Mom," he promised.

"Yes, indeed," Maizie replied.

As well as other things, she added silently as she watched Christopher walk away, anticipation welling in her chest. *Wait until the girls hear about this.*

Chapter One

Okay, how did it get to be so late?

The exasperated, albeit rhetorical, question echoed almost tauntingly in her brain as Lily Langtry hurried through her house, checking to make sure she hadn't left any of her ground-floor windows open or her back door unlocked. There hadn't been any break-ins in her neighborhood, but she lived alone and felt that you could never be too careful.

The minutes felt as if they were racing by.

There was a time when she was not only on time but early for everything from formal appointments to the everyday events that took place in her life. But that was before her mother had passed away, before she was all alone and the only one who was in charge of the details of her life.

It seemed to her that even when she was taking care

of her mother and holding down the two jobs that paying off her mother's medical bills necessitated, she had usually been far more organized and punctual than she was these days. Now that there was only one of her, in essence only one person to be responsible for, her ability to be on top of things seemed to have gone right out the window. If she intended to be ready by eight, in her mind she had to shoot for seven-thirty—and even that didn't always pan out the way she hoped it would.

This morning she'd told herself she would be out the door by seven. It was now eight-ten and she was just stepping into her high heels.

"Finally," she mumbled as she grabbed her bag and launched herself out the front door while simultaneously searching for her keys. The latter were currently eluding detection somewhere within the nether regions of her oversize purse.

Preoccupied, engaged in the frantic hunt that was making her even later than she already was, Lily wasn't looking where she was going.

Which was why she almost stepped on him.

Looking back, in her defense, she hadn't been expecting anything to be on her doorstep, much less a moving black ball of fur that yipped pathetically when her foot came down on his paw.

Jumping backward, Lily's hand went protectively over her chest to contain the heart that felt as if it was about to leap out of it. Lily dropped her purse at the same time.

Containing more things in it than the average overstuffed suitcase, the purse came down with a thud, further frightening the already frightened black ball of fur—which she now saw was a Labrador puppy.

But instead of running, as per the puppy manual, the large-dog-in-training began to lick her shoe.

Since the high heels Lily had selected to wear this morning were open-toe sandals, the upshot was that the puppy was also licking her toes. The end result of that was that the fast-moving little pink tongue was tickling her toes at the same time.

Surprised, stunned, as well as instantly smitten, Lily crouched down to the puppy's level, her demanding schedule temporarily put on hold.

"Are you lost?" she asked the puppy.

Since she was now down to his level, the black Labrador puppy abandoned her shoes and began to lick her face instead. Had there been a hard part to Lily's heart, it would have turned to utter mush as she completely capitulated, surrendering any semblance of control to her unexpected invader.

When she finally rose back up to her feet, Lily looked in both directions along the residential through street where she lived to see if anyone was running up or down the block, frantically searching for a lost pet.

It was apparent that no one was since all she saw was Mr. Baker across the street getting into his midlife-crisis vehicle—a sky-blue Corvette—which he drove to work every morning.

Since it wasn't moving, Lily took no note of the beige sedan parked farther down the block and across the street. Nor did she notice the older woman who was slouched down in the driver's seat.

The puppy appeared to be all alone.

She looked back at the puppy, who was back to licking her shoes. Pulling first one foot back, then the other, she only succeeded in drawing the dog into her house because the Labrador's attention was completely focused on her shoes.

"Looks like your family hasn't realized that you're missing yet," she told the puppy.

The Lab glanced up, cocking his head as if he was hanging on her every word. Lily couldn't help wondering if the animal understood her. She knew people who maintained that dogs only understood commands that had been drilled into their heads, but she had her doubts about that. This one was actually making eye contact and she was *certain* that he was taking in every word.

"I have to go to work," she told her fuzzy, uninvited guest.

The Labrador continued watching her as if she was the only person in the whole world. Lily knew when she'd lost a battle.

She sighed and stepped back even farther into her foyer, allowing the puppy access to her house.

"Oh, all right, you can come in and stay until I get back," she told the puppy, surrendering to the warm brown eyes that were staring up at her so intently.

If she was letting the animal stay here, she had to leave it something to eat and drink, she realized. Turning on her heel, Lily hurried back the kitchen to leave the puppy a few last-minute survival items.

She filled a soup bowl full of water and extracted a few slices of roast béef she'd picked up from the supermarket deli on her way home last night.

Lily placed the latter on a napkin and put both bowl and napkin on the floor.

"This should hold you until I get back," she informed the puppy. Looking down, she saw that the puppy, who she'd just assumed would follow her to a food source, was otherwise occupied. He was busy gnawing on one of the legs of her kitchen chair. "Hey!" she cried. "Stop that!"

The puppy went right on gnawing until she physically separated him from the chair. He looked up at her, clearly confused.

In her house for less than five minutes and the Labrador puppy had already presented her with a dilemma, Lily thought.

"Oh, God, you're teething, aren't you? If I leave you here, by the time I get back it'll look like a swarm of locusts had come through, won't it?" She knew the answer to that one. Lily sighed. It was true what they said, no good deed went unpunished. "Well, you can't stay here, then." Lily looked around the kitchen and the small family room just beyond. Almost all the furniture, except for the TV monitor, was older than she was. "I don't have any money for new furniture."

As if he understood that he was about to be put out again, the puppy looked up at her and then began to whine.

Pathetically.

Softhearted to begin with, Lily found that she was no match for the sad little four-footed fur ball. Closing the door on him would be akin to abandoning the puppy in a snowdrift.

"All right, all right, all right, you can come with me," she cried, giving in. "Maybe someone at work will have a suggestion as to what I can do with you."

Lily stood for a minute, studying the puppy warily. Would it bite her if she attempted to pick it up? Her experience with dogs was limited to the canines she saw on television. After what she'd just witnessed, she knew that she definitely couldn't leave the puppy alone in her house. At the same time, she did have the uneasy feeling that the Labrador wasn't exactly trained to be obedient yet.

Still, trained or not, she felt as if she should at least *try* to get the puppy to follow her instructions. So she walked back over to the front door. The puppy was watching her every move intently, but remained exactly where he was. Lily tried patting her leg three times in short, quick succession. The puppy cocked its head, as if to say, *Now what?*

"C'mon, boy, come here," Lily called to him, patting her leg again, this time a little more urgently. To her relief—as well as surprise—this time the puppy came up to her without any hesitation.

Opening the front door, Lily patted her leg again— and was rewarded with the same response. The puppy came up to her side—the side she'd just patted—his eager expression all but shouting, *Okay, I'm here. Now what?*

Lily currently had no answer for that, but she hoped to within the hour.

"Hey, I don't remember anyone declaring that this was 'bring your pet to work' day," Alfredo Delgado, one of the chefs that Theresa Manetti employed at her catering company, quipped when Lily walked into the storefront office. She was holding a makeshift leash, fashioned out of rope. The black Lab was on the other end of the leash, ready to give the office a thorough investigation the moment the other end of the leash was dropped.

Theresa walked out of her small inner office and regarded the animal, her expression completely unfathomable.

"I'm sorry I'm late," Lily apologized to the woman who wrote out her checks. "I ran into a snag."

"From here it looks like the snag is following you," Theresa observed.

She glanced expectantly at the young woman she'd taken under her wing a little more than a year ago. That was when she'd hired Lily as her pastry chef after discovering that Lily could create delicacies so delicious, they could make the average person weep. But, softhearted woman that she was, Theresa hadn't taken her on because of her skills so much as because Lily's mother had recently passed away, leaving her daughter all alone in the world. Theresa, like her friends Maizie and Cecilia, had a great capacity for sympathy.

Lily flushed slightly now, her cheeks growing a soft shade of pink.

"I'm sorry, he was just there on my doorstep this morning when I opened the door. I couldn't just leave him there to roam the streets. If I came home tonight and found out that someone had run him over, I wouldn't be able to live with myself."

"Why didn't you just leave him at your place?" Alfredo asked, curious. "That's what I would have done." He volunteered this course of action while bending down, scratching the puppy behind its ears.

"I normally would have done that, too," Lily answered. "But there was one thing wrong with that—he apparently sees the world as one giant chew toy."

"So you brought him here," Theresa concluded. It was neither a question nor an accusation, just a statement of the obvious. A bemused smile played on the older woman's lips as she regarded the animal. "Just make sure he stays out of the kitchen."

Lily gestured around the area, hoping Theresa would see things her way. This was all temporary. "Everything here's made out of metal. His little teeth can't do any damage," she pointed out, then looked back at Theresa hopefully. "Can he stay—just for today?" Lily emphasized.

Theresa pretended to think the matter over—as if she hadn't had a hand in the puppy's sudden magical appearance on her pastry chef's doorstep. After Maizie had mentioned that their late friend's son was opening up his animal hospital two doors down from her real estate office and went on to present him as a possible new candidate for their very unique service, Theresa had suggested getting Christopher together with Lily. She'd felt that the young woman could use something positive happening to her and had been of that opinion for a while now.

The search for a way to bring the two together in a so-called "natural" fashion was quick and fruitful when, as a sidebar, Cecilia had casually asked if either she or Maizie knew of anyone looking to adopt a puppy. Her dog, Princess, had given birth to eight puppies six weeks ago, and the puppies needed to be placed before "they start eating me out of house and home," Cecilia had told her friends.

It was as if lightning had struck. Everything had fallen into place after that.

Theresa was aware of Lily's approximate time of departure and had informed Cecilia. The latter proceeded to leave the puppy—deliberately choosing the runt of the litter—on Lily's doorstep. Cecilia left the rambunctious puppy there not once but actually several times before she hit upon the idea of bribing the little dog with a large treat, which she proceeded to embed in the open weave of the welcome mat.

Even so, Cecilia had just barely made it back to her sedan before Lily had swung open her front door.

Once inside the catering shop, the puppy proceeded to make himself at home while he sniffed and investigated every inch of the place.

Lily watched him like a hawk, afraid of what he might do next. In her opinion, Theresa was a wonderful person, but everyone had their breaking point and she didn't want the puppy to find Theresa's.

"Um, Theresa," Lily began as she shooed the puppy away from a corner where a number of boxes were piled up, "how old are your grandchildren now?"

Theresa slanted a deliberately wary look at the younger woman. "Why?"

Lily smiled a little too broadly as she made her sales pitch. "Wouldn't they love to have a puppy? You could surprise them with Jonathan."

Theresa raised an eyebrow quizzically. "Jonathan?" she repeated.

Lily gestured at the Labrador. "The puppy. I had to call him something," she explained.

"You named him. That means you're already attached to him," Alfredo concluded with a laugh, as if it was a done deal.

There was something akin to a panicky look on Lily's face. She didn't want to get attached to anything. She was still trying to get her life on track after losing her mother. Taking on something new—even a pet—was out of the question.

"No, it doesn't," Lily protested. "I just couldn't keep referring to the puppy as 'it.'"

"Sure you could," Alfredo contradicted with a knowing attitude. "That you didn't want to means that you've already bonded with the little ball of flying fur."

"No, no bonding," Lily denied firmly, then made her final argument on the matter. "I don't even know *how* to bond with an animal. The only pet I ever had was a goldfish and Seymour only lived for two days." Which firmly convinced her that she had absolutely no business trying to care for a pet of any kind.

Alfredo obviously didn't see things in the same light that she did. "Then it's high time you got back into the saddle, Lily. You can't accept defeat that easily," he told her.

Finding no support in that quarter, Lily appealed to her boss. "Theresa—"

Theresa placed a hand supportively on the younger woman's shoulder. "I'm with Alfredo on this," she told Lily. "Besides," she pointed out, "you can't give the dog away right now."

"Why not?" Lily asked.

Theresa was the soul of innocence as she explained, "Because his owner might be out looking for him even as we speak."

Lily blew out a breath. She'd forgotten about that. "Good point," she admitted, chagrinned by her oversight. "I'll make flyers and put them up."

"In the meantime," Theresa continued as she thoughtfully regarded the black ball of fur and paws, "I suggest you make sure the little guy's healthy."

"How do I go about doing that?" Lily asked, completely clueless when it came to the care of anything other than humans. She freely admitted to having a brown thumb. Anything that was green and thriving would begin to whither and die under her care—which was why she didn't attempt to maintain a garden anymore. The thought of caring for a pet brought a chill to her spine.

"Well, for starters," Theresa told her, "if I were you I would bring him to a veterinarian."

"A vet?" she looked at the puppy that now appeared to be utterly enamored with Alfredo. The chef was scratching Jonathan behind the ears and along his nose, sending the Labrador to seventh heaven. "He doesn't look sick. Is that really necessary?"

"Absolutely," Theresa answered without a drop of hesitation. "Just think, if someone is looking for him, how would it look if you handed over a sick dog? If they wanted to, they could turn around and sue you for negligence."

Lily felt hemmed in. The last thing she wanted was to have to take care of something, to get involved with a living, breathing entity.

Eyeing the puppy uncertainly, Lily sighed. "I should have never opened the door this morning."

"Oh, how can you say that? Look at this adorable little face," Theresa urged, cupping the puppy's chin and turning his head toward Lily.

"I'm trying not to," Lily answered honestly. But Theresa was right. She didn't want to chance something happening to the puppy while it was temporarily in her care. Emphasis on the word *temporarily,* she thought. "Okay, how do I go about finding an animal doctor who's good, but not expensive? I wouldn't know where to start," she admitted, looking to Theresa for guidance since the woman had been the one to bring up the matter of a vet to begin with.

Theresa's smile bordered on being beatific. "Well, as luck would have it, I happen to know of one who just opened up a new practice a few doors down from one of my best friends. She took her dog to him and told me that he performed nothing short of a miracle on Lazarus." The fact that Maizie didn't have a dog named Lazarus, or a dog named anything else for that matter, was an unimportant, minor detail in the grand scheme of things. As a rule, Theresa didn't lie, but there were times—such as now—when rules were meant to be bent if not altogether broken. "Why don't I call her to get his phone number for you?" she suggested, looking at Lily.

That sounded like as good a plan as any, she supposed. "Sure, why not?" Lily replied with a vague shrug, resigned to this course of action. "What do I have to lose? It's only money, right?"

Theresa knew that times were tight for the younger woman. She saw what she was about to propose as an investment in Lily's future happiness.

"I tell you what. We've had a great month. I'll pay for 'Jonathan's' visit," she offered, petting the eager puppy on the head. The dog stopped roaming around long enough to absorb the head pat and then went back to sniffing the entire area for a second time. "Consider it my gift to you."

"How about me?" Alfredo said, pretending to feel left out. "Got any gifts for me, boss?"

"I'll pay for your visit to the vet, too, if you decide

you need to go," Theresa quipped as she retreated into her office.

Once inside, Theresa carefully closed the door and crossed to her desk. She didn't care for cell phones. The connection was never as clear as a landline in her opinion. Picking up the receiver, she quickly dialed the number she wanted to reach.

Maizie picked up on the second ring. "Connors' Realty."

"Houston, we have liftoff," Theresa announced in what sounded like a stage whisper to her own ear.

"Theresa?" Maizie asked uncertainly. "Is that you?"

"Of course it's me. Who else would call you and say that?"

"I haven't the vaguest idea. Theresa, I mean this in the kindest way, but you've definitely been watching too many movies, woman. Now, what is it that you're trying to say?"

Impatience wove through every word. "That Lily is bringing the puppy to Frances's son."

"Then why didn't you just say so?"

"Because it sounds so ordinary that way," Theresa complained.

"Sometimes, Theresa, ordinary is just fine. Is she bringing the puppy in today?"

"That's what I urged her to do."

"Perfect," Maizie said with heartfelt enthusiasm. "Nothing like being two doors down from young love about to unfold."

"I don't see how that's any different from Houston, we have liftoff," Theresa protested.

"Maybe it's not, Theresa," Maizie conceded, not because she thought she was wrong, but because she knew Theresa liked to be right. "Maybe it's not."

Chapter Two

The first thing that struck Christopher when he walked into Exam Room 3 was that the woman was standing rather than sitting. She was clearly uneasy in her present situation. The puppy with her appeared to have the upper hand.

Smiling at her, he made a quick assessment before he spoke. "This isn't your dog, is it?"

Lily looked at the veterinarian, stunned. "How can you tell?" she asked.

All she had given the receptionist out front was her name. The dark-haired woman had immediately nodded and told her that "Mrs. Manetti called to say you'd be coming in." The young woman at the desk, Erika, had then proceeded to call over one of the veterinary aides, who promptly ushered her and Jonathan into an exam room. As far as she knew, no details about her nonrelationship to the animal she'd brought in had been given.

Maybe she was wrong, Lily realized belatedly.

"Did Theresa tell you that?" she asked.

"Theresa?" Christopher repeated, confused.

Okay, wrong guess, Lily decided. She shook her head. "Never mind," she told him, then repeated her initial question. "How can you tell he's not mine?" Was there some sort of look that pet owners had? Some sort of inherent sign that the civilian non–pet owners obviously seemed to lack?

Christopher nodded toward the antsy puppy who looked as if he was ready to race around all four of the exam room's corners almost simultaneously. "He has a rope around his neck," Christopher pointed out.

He probably equated that with cruelty to animals, Lily thought. "Necessity is the mother of invention," she told him, then explained her thinking. "I made a loop and tied a rope to it because I didn't have any other way to make sure that he would follow me."

There was a stirring vulnerability about the young woman with the long, chestnut hair. It pulled him in. Christopher looked at her thoughtfully, taking care not to allow his amusement at her action to show. Some people were thin-skinned and would construe that as being laughed at. Nothing could have been further from the truth.

"No leash," he concluded.

"No leash," Lily confirmed. Then, because she thought that he needed more information to go on— and she had no idea what was and wasn't important when it came to assessing the health of a puppy—she went on to tell the good-looking vet, "I found him on my doorstep—I tripped over him, actually."

The way she said it led Christopher to his next conclusion. "And I take it that you don't know who he belongs to?"

"No, I don't. If I did," Lily added quickly, "I would have brought him back to his owner. But I've never seen him before this morning."

"Then how do you know the dog's name is Jonathan?" As far as he could see, the puppy had no dog tags.

She shrugged almost as if she was dismissing the question. "I don't."

Christopher looked at her a little more closely. Okay, he thought, something was definitely off here. "When you brought him in, you told my receptionist that his name was Jonathan."

"That's what I call him," she responded quickly, then explained, "I didn't want to just refer to him as 'puppy' or 'hey, you' so I gave him a name." The young woman shrugged and the simple gesture struck him as being somewhat hapless. "He seems to like it. At least he looks up at me when I call him by that name."

Christopher didn't want her being under the wrong impression, even if there was no real harm in thinking that way.

"The right intonation does that," he told Lily. "I'll let you in on a secret," Christopher went on, lowering his voice as if this was a guarded confession he was about to impart. "He'd respond to 'Refrigerator' if you said it the same way."

To prove his point, Christopher moved around the exam table until he was directly behind the puppy.

Once there, he called, "Refrigerator!" and Jonathan turned his head around to look at him, taking a few follow-up steps in order to better see who was calling him.

His point proven, Christopher glanced at the woman. "See?"

She nodded, but in Christopher's opinion the woman appeared more overwhelmed than convinced. He had been born loving animals, and as far back as he could remember, his world had been filled with critters large and small. He had an affinity for them, something that his mother had passed on to him.

He was of the mind that everyone should have a pet and that pets improved their owners' quality of life—as well as vice versa.

"Just how long have you and Jonathan been together?" he asked. His guess was that it couldn't have been too long because she and the puppy hadn't found their proper rhythm yet.

Lily glanced at her watch before she answered the vet. "In ten minutes it'll be three hours—or so," she replied.

"Three hours," he repeated.

"Or so," she added in a small voice. Christopher paused for a moment. Studying the petite, attractive young woman before him, his eyes crinkled with the smile that was taking over his face.

"You've never had a dog before, have you?" The question was rhetorical. He should have seen this from the very start. The woman definitely did not seem at ease around the puppy.

"It shows?" She didn't know which she felt more, surprised or embarrassed by the question.

"You look like you're afraid of Jonathan," he told her.

"I'm not," she protested with a bit too much feeling. Then, when the vet made no comment but continued looking at her, she dialed her defensiveness back a little. "Well, not entirely." And then, after another beat, she amended that by saying, "He's cute and everything, but he has these teeth…"

Christopher suppressed a laugh. "Most dogs do. At least," he corrected himself, thinking of a neglected dog he'd treated at the city's animal shelter just the other day, "the healthy ones do."

She wasn't expressing herself correctly, Lily realized. But then, communication was sometimes hard for her. Her skill lay in the pastries she created, not in getting her thoughts across to people she didn't know.

Lily tried again. "But Jonathan's always biting,"

"There's a reason for that. He's teething," Christopher told her. "When I was a kid, I had a cousin like that," he confided. "Chewed on everything and everyone until all his baby teeth came in."

As if to illustrate what he was saying, she saw the puppy attempt to sink his teeth into the vet's hand. Instead of yelping, Christopher laughed, rubbed the Labrador's head affectionately. Before Jonathan could try to bite him a second time, the vet pulled a rubber squeaky toy out of his lab coat pocket. Distracted, Jonathan went after the toy—a lime-green octopus with wiggly limbs.

High-pitched squeaks filled the air in direct proportion to the energy the puppy was expending chewing on his new toy.

Just for a second, there was a touch of envy in her eyes when she raised them to his face, Christopher thought. Her cheeks were also turning a very light shade of pink.

"You probably think I'm an idiot," Lily told him.

The last thing he wanted was for her to think he was judging her—harshly or otherwise. But he could admit he was attracted to her.

"What I think," he corrected, "is that you might need a little help and guidance here."

Oh, God, yes, she almost exclaimed out loud, managing to bite the gush of words back at the last moment. Instead, she asked hopefully, "You have a book for me to read?"

Christopher inclined his head. He had something a little more personal and immediate in mind. "If you'd like to read one, I have several I could recommend," he conceded. "But personally, I've always found it easier when I had something visual to go on."

"Like a DVD?" she asked, not altogether sure what he meant by his statement.

Christopher grinned. "More like a *P-E-R-S-O-N.*"

For just a second, Lily found herself getting caught up in the vet's grin. Something akin to a knot—or was that a butterfly?—twisted around in her stomach. Rousing herself, Lily blinked, certain that she'd somehow misunderstood the veterinarian.

From his handsome, dimpled face, to his dirty-blond hair, to his broad shoulders, the man was a symphony of absolute charm and she was rather accustomed to being almost invisible around people who came across so dynamically. The more vibrant they were, the more understated she became, as if she was shrinking in the sunlight of their effervescence.

Given that, it seemed almost implausible to her that

Christopher was saying what it sounded as if he was saying. But in the interest of clarity, she had to ask, "Are you volunteering to help me with the dog?"

To her surprise, rather than appearing annoyed or waving away the question entirely, he laughed. "If you have to ask, I must be doing it wrong, but yes, I'm volunteering." Then he backtracked slightly as if another thought had occurred to him. "Unless, of course, your husband or boyfriend or significant other has some objections to my mentoring you through the hallowed halls of puppy ownership."

Her self-image—that of being a single person—was so ingrained in her that Lily just assumed she came across that way. That the vet made such a stipulation seemed almost foreign to her.

"There's no husband or boyfriend or significant other to object to anything," she informed the man.

She was instantly rewarded with the flash of another dimpled grin. "Oh, well then, unless you have any objections, I can accompany you to the local dog park this weekend for some pointers."

She hadn't even been aware that there was a dog park anywhere, much less one here in Bedford, but she kept that lack of knowledge to herself.

"Although," the vet was saying, "I do have one thing to correct already."

Lily braced herself for criticism as she asked, "What am I doing wrong?"

Christopher shook his head. "Not you, me," he told her affably. "I just said puppy ownership."

She was still in the dark as to where this was going. "Yes, I know, I heard you."

"Well, that's actually wrong," he told her. "That

phrase would indicate that you owned the puppy when in reality—"

"The puppy owns me?" she guessed. Where else could he be headed with this? She could very easily see the puppy taking over.

But Christopher shook his head. "You own each other, and sometimes even those lines get a little blurred," he admitted, then went on to tell her, "You do it right and your pet becomes part of your family and you become part of his family."

For a moment, Lily forgot to resist experiencing the exact feelings that the vet was talking about. Instead, just for that one sliver of time, she allowed herself to believe that she was part of something larger than just herself, and it promised to ease the loneliness she was so acutely aware of whenever she wasn't at work.

Whenever she left the people she worked with and returned to her house and her solitary existence.

The next moment, she forced herself to lock down and pull back, retreating into the Spartan world she'd resided in ever since she'd lost her mother.

"That sounds like something I once read in a children's book," she told him politely.

"Probably was," Christopher willingly conceded. "Children see the world far more honestly than we do. They don't usually have to make up excuses or search for ways to explain away what they feel—they just *feel*," he said with emphasis as well as no small amount of admiration.

And then he got back to the business at hand. "Since you can count the length of your relationship with Jonathan in hours, I take it that means you have no information regarding his rather short history."

She shook her head. "None whatsoever, I'm afraid," she confessed.

Christopher took it all in stride. He turned his attention to his four-footed patient. "Well, I'm making a guess as to his age—"

Curious about the sort of procedures that involved, she asked, "How can you do that?"

"His teeth," Christopher pointed out. "The same teeth he's been trying out on you," he added with an indulgent smile that seemed incredibly sexy to her. "He's got his baby teeth. He appears to be a purebred Labrador, so there aren't any stray factors to take into account regarding his size and growth pattern. Given his teeth and the size of his paws in comparison to the rest of him, I'd say he's no more than five or six weeks old. And I think I can also safely predict that he's going to be a *very* large dog, given the size of the paws he's going to grow into," the vet concluded.

She looked down at the puppy. Jonathan seemed to be falling all over himself in an attempt to engage the vet's attention. No matter which way she sliced it, the puppy *was* cute—as long as he wasn't actively biting her.

"Well, I guess that's something I'm not going to find out," she murmured, more to herself than to the man on the other side of the exam table.

Christopher watched her with deep curiosity in his eyes. "Do you mind if I ask why not?"

"No."

"No?" he repeated, not really certain what the answer pertained to.

Her mind was *really* working in slow motion today,

Lily thought, upbraiding herself. "I mean no, I don't mind you asking."

When there was no further information following that up, he coaxed, "And the answer to my question is—?"

"Oh."

More blushing accompanied the single-syllable word. She really was behaving like the proverbial village idiot. Lily upbraided herself. What in heaven's name had come over her? It was like her brain had been dipped in molasses and couldn't rinse itself off in order to return to its normal speed—or even the bare semblance of going half-speed.

"Because as soon as I leave here with Jonathan, I'm going to make some flyers and post them around town," she told the vet. She was rather a fair sketch artist when she put her mind to it and planned to create a likeness of this puppy to use on the poster. "Somebody's got to be out looking for him."

"If you're not planning on keeping him, why did you bring him in to be examined?"

She would have thought that he, as a vet, would have thought the reason was self-explanatory. She told him anyway.

"Well, I didn't want to take a chance that there might be something wrong with him. I wouldn't want to neglect taking care of something just because I wasn't keeping it," she answered.

"So you're like a drive-by Good Samaritan?"

She shrugged off what might have been construed as a compliment. From her point of view, there was really nothing to compliment. She was only doing what anyone else in her place would do—if they had any kind of a conscience, Lily silently qualified.

Out loud, she merely replied, "Yes, something like that."

"I guess 'Jonathan' here was lucky it was your front step he picked to camp out on." He crouched down to the dog's level. "Aren't you, boy?" he asked with affection, stroking the puppy's head again.

As before, the dog reacted with enthusiasm, driving the top of his head into the vet's hand as well as leaning in to rub his head against Christopher's side.

Watching the puppy, Lily thought that the Labrador was trying to meld with the vet.

"Tell you what," Christopher proposed after giving the puppy a quick examination and rising back up again, "since he seems healthy enough, why don't we hold off until after this weekend before continuing with this exam? Then, if no one responds to your 'found' flyers, you bring Jonathan here back and I'll start him out on his series of immunizations."

"Immunizations?" Lily questioned.

By the sound of her voice, it seemed to Christopher that the shapely young woman hadn't given that idea any thought at all. But then she'd admitted that she'd never had a pet before, so her lack of knowledge wasn't really that unusual.

"Dogs need to be immunized, just like kids," he told her.

Somewhere in the back of her mind, a stray fact fell into place. She recalled having heard that once or twice. "Right," she murmured.

Christopher smiled in response to her tacit agreement. "And," he continued, "if you don't get a call from a frantic owner by this weekend, why don't we make a date to meet at the park on Sunday, say about eleven o'clock?" he further suggested.

"A date," she echoed.

Given the way her eyes had widened, the word *date* was not the one he should have used, Christopher realized. It had been carelessly thrown out there on his part.

Very smoothly, Christopher extricated himself from what could potentially be a very sticky situation. "Yes, but I have a feeling that Jonathan might not be comfortable with my advertising the situation, so for simplicity's sake—and possibly to save Jonathan's reputation," he amended with a wink that had her stomach doing an unexpected jackknife dive off the high board—again, "why don't we just call the meeting a training session?"

Training session.

That phrase conjured up an image that involved a great deal of work. "You'd do that?" she asked incredulously.

"Call it a training session? Sure."

"No, I mean actually volunteer to show me how to train Jonathan—provided I still have him," she qualified.

"I thought that part was clear," Christopher said with a smile.

But Lily had already moved on to another question. "Why?"

"Why did I think that was clear?" he guessed. "Because I couldn't say it any more straightforwardly than that."

She really *did* need to learn how to express herself

better. "No, I mean why would you volunteer to show me how to train the dog?"

"Because, from personal experience, I know that living with an untrained dog can be hell—for both the dog and the person. Training the dog is just another name for mutual survival," he told her.

"But aren't you busy?" she asked him, feeling guilty about taking the vet away from whatever he had planned for the weekend. Grateful though she was, she wondered if she came across that needy or inept to him.

Christopher thought of the unopened boxes that were throughout his house—and had been for the past three months—waiting to be emptied and their contents put away. He'd moved back into his old home, never having gotten around to selling it after his mother had passed away. Now it only seemed like the natural place to return to. But the boxes were taunting him. Helping this woman find her footing with the overactive puppy gave him a good excuse to procrastinate a little longer.

"No more than the average human being," he told her.

"If the dog is still with me by the weekend," she prefaced, "I still can't pay you for the training session. At least, not all at once. But we could arrange for some sort of a payment schedule," she suggested, not wanting to seem ungrateful.

"I don't remember asking to be paid," Christopher pointed out.

"Then why would you go out of your way like that to help me?" she asked, bewildered.

"Call it earning a long-overdue merit badge."

She opened her mouth to protest that she wasn't a

charity case, but just then one of his assistants knocked on the door.

"Doctor, your patients are piling up," she said through the door.

"I'll be right there," he told the assistant, then turned to Lily. "I'll see you at the dog park on Sunday at eleven," he said. "Oh, and if you have any questions, don't hesitate to call. I can be reached here during the day and on my cell after hours."

"You take calls after hours?" Lily asked him, surprised.

"I've found that pets, like kids, don't always conveniently get sick between the hours of eight and six," he told her, opening the door.

"Wait, how much do I owe you for today?" she asked, forgetting that there was a receptionist at the front desk who would most likely be the one taking care of any and all charges for today's visit.

Christopher started to head out. He could hear his next patient barking impatiently from all the way down the hall. Without breaking stride, he told Lily, "I don't charge for conversations."

He was gone before she could protest and remind him that he *had* given Jonathan a cursory examination.

Chapter Three

Lily was certain she hadn't heard the man correctly. Granted, Jonathan hadn't received any shots or had any specimens taken for a lab workup, but the veterinarian *had* spent at least twenty minutes talking to her about the puppy and he *had* looked the Labrador over. In her book, that sort of thing had to constitute an "office visit."

Didn't it?

While she was more than willing to do favors for people, Lily had never liked being on the receiving end of a favor because it put her in the position of owing someone something. She was grateful to the vet for taking an interest in the puppy that was temporarily in her care and she was happy that he'd offered to instruct her on how to maintain a peaceful coexistence with the ball of fur while the puppy *was* in her care, but she wasn't about to accept any of that for free.

It wouldn't be right.

Taking a breath, Lily extracted her checkbook from her jumbled purse and then braced herself for her next confrontation with the puppy.

Doing her best to sound stern, or at least authoritative, she looked down at Jonathan and said, "We're going out now, Jonathan. Try not to yank me all over this time, all right?"

If the puppy understood what she was asking, then he chose to ignore it because the minute she opened the door, he all but flew out. Since the rope she had tethered to the Labrador was currently also wrapped around her hand, the puppy, perforce, came to an abrupt, almost comical halt two seconds later. He'd run out of slack.

The puppy gave her what seemed to Lily to be a reproving look—if puppies could look at someone reprovingly.

Maybe she was reading too much into it, Lily told herself.

Still, she felt compelled to tell the puppy, "I asked you not to run."

Making her way out to the front of the clinic, Lily saw the receptionist, Erika, looking at her. She flushed a little in response. "You probably think I'm crazy, talking to the dog."

Erika's dark eyes sparkled. "On the contrary, most pet owners would think you're crazy if you didn't. They understand us," she explained with easy confidence, nodding toward Jonathan. "They just sometimes choose not to listen. In that way, they're really no different than kids," Erika added. "Except that pets are probably more loyal in the long run."

"I'm not planning for a 'long run,'" Lily told the receptionist. "I'm just minding this puppy until his owner turns up to claim him," she explained. Placing her checkbook on her side of the counter, she opened it to the next blank check, then took out her pen. All the while, Jonathan was tugging on the rope, trying to separate himself from her. "Okay, how much do I make the check out for?" She flashed a somewhat shy smile at the receptionist. "I warn you, it might be slightly illegible."

Jonathan was tugging on his makeshift leash, desperately wanting to escape from the clinic—and in all likelihood, from her, as well. Legible writing under those circumstances went out the window.

Erika glanced at the paperwork that had just been sent to her computer monitor a moment ago. She looked up at the woman on the other side of her desk. "Nothing," she answered.

That couldn't be right. Could the vet really have been serious about not charging her? "For the visit," Lily prompted.

"Nothing," Erika repeated.

"But Dr. Whitman saw the dog," Lily protested.

Erika looked at the screen again.

"Well, he's not charging you for seeing the dog," Erika told her. "But now that I look, I see that he does have one thing written down here," the receptionist informed her, reading the column marked "special instructions."

Lily could feel her arm being elongated by the second. For a little guy, the Labrador was uncommonly strong in her opinion. She tugged him back. "What?" she asked the receptionist.

Instead of answering her immediately, Erika said, "Just a minute," and opened the large side drawer. She started rummaging through it. It took her a minute to locate what she was searching for.

"Dr. Whitman wants me to give you this."

"This" turned out to be not one thing but two things. One item was a small, bright blue braided collar made to fit the neck of a dog just about the puppy's size and the other was a matching bright blue braided leash.

Erika placed both on the counter in front of Jonathan's keeper.

"It's a collar and leash," Erika prompted when the woman with Jonathan continued just to look at the two items. "Dr. Whitman has a 'thing' against ropes. He's afraid that a pet might wind up choking itself," she confided.

Given the Labrador's propensity for dashing practically in two directions at the same time, getting a sturdy leash that wouldn't bite into his tender throat did make sense to her, Lily thought. She certainly wasn't about to refuse to accept the collar and leash.

"Okay, so what do I owe you for the collar and leash?" she asked.

The answer turned out to be the same. "Nothing," Erika replied.

She'd heard of nonprofit, but this was ridiculous. "They have to cost *something,*" Lily insisted.

All of her life, she'd had to pay, and sometimes pay dearly, for everything she had ever needed or used. Taking something, whether it involved a service that was rendered or an item that was given to her, without the benefit of payment just didn't seem right to Lily. It also offended her sense of independence.

"Just pennies," Erika told her. When she looked at the young woman skeptically, the receptionist explained, "Dr. Whitman orders them practically by the crate full. He likes to give them out. Just think of it as a gesture of goodwill," Erika advised.

What she thought of it as was a gesture of charity placing her in debt, however minor the act seemed to the vet.

Lily tried one last time. "You're sure I can't pay you, make a contribution to your needy-dog fund, *something?*"

"I'm sure," Erika replied. She pointed to her monitor as if to drive the point home. "It says right here, 'no charge.'" The woman hit two keys and the printer on the stand behind her came to life, spitting out a hard copy of what was on her monitor. She handed what amounted to a nonreceipt to the puppy's keeper. "See?" Erika asked with a smile.

Lily took the single sheet of paper. Unable to pay for either the office visit or the two items now in her possession, all she could do was say thank you—which she did.

"No problem," Erika replied. She got up from her desk and came around to the other side, where the Labrador stood fiercely yanking against the rope.

"Why don't I put the collar on him while you try to hold him in place?" Erika suggested. "This way, he won't make a break for it."

"You're a godsend," Lily said with a relieved sigh. She'd been wondering just how to manage to exchange the rope for the collar and leash she'd just been given without having the puppy make a mad dash for freedom.

"No, just an animal clinic receptionist who's been at it for a while," Erika corrected modestly.

She had the collar on the puppy and the leash connected to it within a couple of minutes. Only at that point did she undo the rope. The next moment, the rope hung limp and useless in Lily's hand.

Lily was quick to leave it on the desk.

Standing up, Erika told her, "You're ready to go." The words were no sooner out of her mouth than Jonathan made an urgent, insistent beeline for the front door. "I think Jonathan agrees," Erika said with a laugh. "Here, I'll hold the door open for you," she offered, striding quickly over to it.

The instant the door was opened and no longer presented an obstacle, the dog made a break for the outside world and freedom. Lily was nearly thrown off balance as he took her with him.

"Bye!" she called out, tossing the words over her shoulder as she trotted quickly in the dog's wake, trying hard to keep up and even harder to keep from falling. Jonathan seemed oblivious to any and all attempts to rein him in.

Erika shook her head as she closed the door and went back to her desk. "I give them two weeks. A month, tops," she murmured to herself.

The second she and her energetic, furry companion returned to Theresa's catering shop, Lily found herself surrounded by everyone she worked with. They were all firing questions at her regarding Jonathan's visit to the new animal hospital. He was the center of attention and appeared to be enjoying himself, barking and licking the hands that were reaching out to pet him.

To her amazement, Lily discovered that of the small band of people who worked for Theresa's catering company, she was the only one who had never had a pet—if she discounted the two-day period, twenty years ago, during which time she had a live goldfish.

Consequently, while keeping Jonathan out of the kitchen area for practical reasons that in no small way involved the Board of Health's regulations, the puppy was allowed to roam freely about the rest of the storefront office. As a result, Jonathan was petted, played with, cooed over and fed unsparingly by everyone, including Theresa. He became the company's mascot in a matter of minutes.

Because their next catering event wasn't until the next evening, the atmosphere within the shop wasn't as hectic and tense as it could sometimes get. Alfredo and his crew were still in the planning and preparation stages for the next day's main menu. Zack Collins, Theresa's resident bartender, was out purchasing the wines and alcoholic beverages that were to be served at the celebration, and Lily was in the semifinal preparation stage, planning just what desserts to create for the occasion.

Checking on everyone's progress, Theresa observed that Lily was doing more than just planning. She was also baking a tray of what appeared to be lighter-than-air crème-filled pastries.

"Did you decide to do a dry run?" Theresa asked, coming up to the young woman.

"In a manner of speaking," Lily replied. Then, because Theresa was more like a mother to her than a boss, Lily paused for a moment and told the woman what was on her mind. "You know that vet you had me bring Jonathan to?"

Theresa's expression gave nothing away, even as her mind raced around, bracing for a problem or some sort of a hiccup in Maizie's plan.

"Yes?"

"He wouldn't let me pay him for the visit," Lily concluded with a perturbed frown.

"Really?" Theresa did her best to infuse the single word with surprise and wonder—rather than the triumphant pleasure, laced with hope, she was experiencing.

"Really," Lily repeated. "I don't like owing people," she continued.

"Honey, sometimes you just have to graciously accept things from other people," Theresa began. But Lily interrupted her.

"I know. That's why I'm doing this," she told Theresa, gesturing at the tray she'd just taken out of the oven. "I thought that since he was nice enough to 'gift' me with his knowledge by checking out Jonathan, I should return the favor and 'gift' him with what I do best."

By now, Theresa was all but beaming. Maizie had gotten it right again, she couldn't help thinking.

"Sounds perfectly reasonable to me," Theresa agreed. She glanced at her watch. It was getting to be close to four o'clock. Maizie had mentioned that Christopher closed the doors to the animal clinic at six. She didn't want Lily to miss encountering the vet. "Since we're not actively catering anything today, why don't you take a run back to the animal clinic and bring that vet your pastries while they're still warm from the oven?" Theresa suggested.

Lily flashed her boss a grateful smile since she was perfectly willing to do just that. But first she had to take care of a more-than-minor detail.

Lily looked around. "Where's Jonathan?"

"Meghan's keeping him occupied," Theresa assured her, referring to one of the servers she had in her permanent employ. In a pinch, the young, resourceful blonde also substituted as a bartender when Zack was otherwise occupied or unavailable. "Why?" She smiled broadly. "Are you worried about him?"

"I just didn't want to leave the puppy here on his own while I make a run to the vet's office." She didn't want to even *begin* to tally the amount of damage the little puppy could do in a very short amount of time.

"He's not on his own," Theresa contradicted. "There are approximately eight sets of eyes on that dog at all times. If anything, he might become paranoid. Go, bring your thank-you pastries to the vet. Sounds as if he might just have earned them," the older woman speculated.

At the last moment, Lily looked at her hesitantly. "If you don't mind," Lily qualified.

"I wouldn't be pushing you out the door if I minded," Theresa pointed out. "Now shoo!" she ordered, gesturing the pastry chef out the door.

She was gone before Theresa could finish saying the last word.

When the bell announced the arrival of yet another patient, Christopher had to consciously refrain from releasing a loud sigh. It wasn't that he minded seeing patients, because he didn't. He enjoyed it, even when he was being challenged or confounded by a pet's condition. Plus, his new practice took all his time, which he didn't mind. It was paperwork that he hated. Paperwork of any kind was tedious, even though he readily admitted that it needed to be done.

Which was why he had two different receptionists, one in the morning, one in the afternoon, to do the inputting and to keep track of things.

However, on occasion, when one or the other was away for longer than ten minutes, he took over and manned the desk, so to speak.

That was what he was currently doing because Erika had taken a quick run to the local take-out place in order to buy and bring back dinner for the office. He looked up from the keyboard to see just who had entered.

"You're back," Christopher said with surprise when he saw Lily coming in. The moment she stepped inside, she filled the waiting area with her unconscious, natural sexiness. Before he knew it, he found himself under her spell. "Is something wrong with Jonathan?" It was the first thing that occurred to him.

And then he noticed that she was carrying a rectangular pink cardboard box. Another animal to examine? No, that couldn't be it. There were no air holes punched into the box, which would mean, under normal circumstances, that it wasn't some stray white mouse or rat she was bringing to him.

"You brought me another patient?" he asked a little warily.

"What?" She saw that he was eyeing the box in her hand and realized belatedly what he had to be thinking. "Oh, this isn't anything to examine," she told him. "At least, not the way you mean."

He had no idea what that meant.

By now, the savory aroma wafting out of the box had reached him and he could feel his taste buds coming to attention.

"What *is* that?" he asked her, leaving the shelter of the reception desk and coming closer. He thought he detected the scent of cinnamon, among other things. "That aroma is nothing short of fantastic."

Lily smiled broadly. "Thank you."

He looked at her in confused surprise. "Is that you?" he asked, slightly bemused.

Was that some sort of new cologne, meant to arouse a man's appetites, the noncarnal variety? He could almost *feel* his mouth watering.

"Only in a manner of speaking," Lily replied with a laugh. When Christopher looked even further confused, she took pity on him and thrust the rectangular box at him. "These are for you—and your staff," she added in case he thought she was singling him out and trying to flirt with him—although she was certain he probably had to endure the latter on a regular basis. Men as good-looking as Christopher Whitman *never* went unnoticed. From his thick, straight dirty-blond hair, to his tall, lean body, to his magnetic blue eyes that seemed to look right *into* her, the man stood out in any crowd.

"It's just my small way of saying thank you," she added.

"You bought these for us?" Christopher asked, taking the box from her.

"No," Lily corrected, "I *made* these for you. I'm a

pastry chef," she explained quickly, in case he thought she was just someone who had slapped together the first dessert recipe she came across on the internet. She wasn't altogether sure what prompted her, but she wanted him to know that in her own way she was a professional, too. "I work for a catering company," she added, then thought that she was probably blurting out more details than the man wanted to hear. "Anyway, since you wouldn't let me pay you, I wanted to do something nice for you. It's all-natural," she told him. "No artificial additives, no gluten, no nuts," she added, in case he was allergic to them the way her childhood best friend had been. "It's all perfectly safe," she assured him.

"Well, it smells absolutely terrific." He opened the box and the aroma seemed to literally swirl all around him. "If I didn't know any better, I would have thought I'd died and gone to heaven," he told her.

"I'm told it tastes even better than it smells," she said rather shyly.

"Let's see if they're right." Christopher took out a pastry and slowly bit into it, as if afraid to disturb its delicate composition. His eyes widened and filled with pleasure. "Heaven has been confirmed," he told her before giving in and taking a second bite.

And then a third.

Chapter Four

Despite the fact that she really was enjoying watching the veterinarian consume the pastry she'd made, Lily did feel a little awkward just standing there. Any second now, someone would either come in with a pet that needed attention, or one of the doctor's assistants would emerge and the moment she was experiencing, watching him, would vanish.

It would be better all around if she left right now.

"Well, I just wanted to drop those off with you," Lily said, waving a hand toward the contents of the opened pink box. With that, she began to walk out of the clinic.

Christopher's mouth was presently occupied, involved in a love affair with the last bite of the pastry that he'd selected. Not wanting to rush the process, he also didn't want Lily to leave just yet. He held up his hand, mutely indicating that he wanted her to stay a moment longer.

"Wait." He managed to voice the urgent request just before he swallowed the last bite he'd taken.

Lily stopped just short of the front door. She shifted slightly as she waited for the vet to be able to speak, all the while wondering just why he would ask her to remain. Was he going to tell her that he'd changed his mind about charging her for today? Or had the man had second thoughts about his offer to meet her in the dog park on Sunday?

And why was she suddenly experiencing this feeling of dread if it was the latter?

"You really made these?" Christopher asked once he'd regained the use of his mouth.

"Yes," she answered slowly, her eyes on his as she tried to fathom why he would think that she would make something like that up.

Unable to resist, Christopher popped the last piece into his mouth. It was gone in the blink of an eye. Gone, but definitely not forgotten.

"They're fantastic," he told her with feeling. Executing magnificent restraint, he forced himself to close the rectangular box. "Do you do this professionally?" he asked. "Like at a restaurant? Do you work for a restaurant?" he rephrased, realizing that his momentary bout of sheer ecstasy had temporarily robbed him of the ability to form coherent questions.

"I work for a caterer," Lily corrected. "But someday, I'd like to open up a bakery of my own," she added before she could think better of it. The man was only making conversation. He didn't want her to launch into a long monologue, citing her future plans.

Christopher nodded and smiled warmly as he lifted the lid on the box just a crack again. There was a little dab of cream on one side. He scraped it off with his fingertip which in turn disappeared between his lips as he savored this last tiny bit.

He looked like a man who had reached Nirvana, Lily couldn't help thinking. A warm, pleased feeling began to spread all through her. Lily forgot to be nervous or uncomfortable.

"You'd have standing room only," Christopher assured her. "What do you call these?" he asked, indicating the pastries that were still in the box.

She hadn't given the matter all that much thought. She recalled what Theresa had called them the first time she'd sampled one. "Bits of Heaven."

Christopher's smile deepened as he nodded his approval. He turned to face her completely as he said, "Good name."

That was when she saw it. The tiny dot of white cream just on the inside corner of his lips. Obviously not all of the dessert had made it *into* his mouth. She thought of ignoring it, certain that the more he spoke, the more likely that the cream would eventually disappear one way or another.

But she didn't want him to be embarrassed by having one of his patients' owners point out that his appearance was less than perfect.

"Um, Dr. Whitman," she began, completely at a loss as to how to proceed. She'd always felt out of sync pointing out someone else's flaws or shortcomings. But this was because she'd brought in the pastries so technically the remnants of cream on his face was her fault.

"Your pastry just made love to my mouth, I think you can call me Chris," Christopher told her, hoping to dismantle some of the barriers that this woman seemed to have constructed around herself.

"Chris," Lily repeated as she tried to begin again.

He liked the sound of his name on Lily's tongue. His smile reflected it. "Yes?"

"You have a little cream on your lip. Well, just below your lip," she amended. Rather than point to the exact location on his face, she pointed to it on hers. "No, the other side," she coached when he'd reversed sides to start with. When Christopher managed to find the spot on his second try, she nodded, relieved. "You got it."

Amused, Christopher was about to say something to her, but he was stopped by the bell over the door. It rang, announcing the arrival of his next patient: a Himalayan cat who looked none too happy about being in a carrier, or about her forced visit to the animal hospital for that matter.

The cat's mistress, a rather matronly-looking brunette with a sunny smile, sighed with relief as she set the carrier down on the floor next to the front desk. "Cedrick is *not* a happy camper today," she said, stating the obvious. Then, before Christopher could turn to the cat's file, the woman prompted, "Cedrick's here for his shots."

That was definitely her cue to leave, Lily thought. She'd stayed too long as it was. Theresa's people were watching Jonathan, but she had a feeling that she was on borrowed time as far as that was concerned.

"Well, bye," she called out to Christopher as she opened the door for herself.

She was surprised to hear his voice following her out of the office as he called, "Don't forget Sunday."

The butterflies she'd just become aware of turned into full-size Rodans in a blink of an eye.

Lily darted out of the office and hurried to her vehicle.

"You look like someone's chasing you," Theresa observed when she all but burst through the front door of the catering shop. "Is everything all right?" the older woman asked.

"Fine. It's fine," Lily answered a little too quickly.

Theresa opted to leave her answer unchallenged, asking instead, "How did he like your pastries?" When Lily looked at her blankly, her expression not unlike that of a deer caught in the headlights, Theresa prompted helpfully, "The vet, how did he like the pastries that you made for him?"

"Oh, that. He liked them," Lily answered. "Sorry, I'm a little preoccupied," she apologized. "I'm thinking about the desserts for tomorrow night's event," she explained. Because she always wanted everything to be perfect—her way of showing Theresa how grateful she was to the woman for taking such an interest in her—she was constantly reviewing what she planned on creating for any given event.

This time it was Theresa who waved a hand, waving away Lily's apology. She was far more interested in the topic she had raised.

"Well, what did he say?" she asked. "Honestly, child, sometimes getting information out of you is just like pulling teeth." Drawing her over to the side, she repeated her request. "Tell me what he said."

She could feel her eyes crinkling as she smiled, recalling the exact words. "That he thought he'd died and gone to heaven."

Theresa nodded in approval. "At least he has taste," she said more to herself than to Lily. Maizie had come up with a good candidate, she couldn't help thinking. "It's an omen," she decided, giving Lily's hand a squeeze. "We'll go with Bits of Heaven for the celebration tomorrow night." And then, because Lily didn't seem to be inclined to say anything further about Christopher for now, she changed topics. "By the way, if you're wondering where Jonathan is, Meghan took him out for a walk. Until he gets housebroken, one of us is going to have to take him out every hour until he finally goes," Theresa advised.

Utterly unaccustomed to anything that had to do with having a pet, Lily looked at her, momentarily confused. "Goes? Goes where? You mean with his owner?" she guessed.

Theresa suppressed a laugh. "No, I meant as in him relieving himself. Unless made to understand otherwise, that puppy is going to think the whole world is his bathroom."

Lily looked at her in complete horror. "Oh, God, I didn't think of that."

"Don't beat yourself up, Lily," Theresa told her kindly, putting her arm around her protégé's shoulders. "You've never had a pet before." Then, to further ease the young woman's discomfort, Theresa told her, "There were always dogs around when I was growing up. This is all like second nature to me."

If she felt that way, maybe there was a chance that she could convince her boss to take the puppy if no one came forward to claim him. Lily gave it one more try. "Are you sure that you don't want to—"

Immediately aware where this was going, Theresa deftly headed it off. "Not a chance. My Siamese would take one look at Jonathan and scratch his eyes out, then go on strike and not eat her food for a week just to make me suffer. As long as that prima donna resides with me, I can't have any other four-footed creatures coming within a yard of the house." Theresa gave her a sympathetic smile. "I'm afraid that until you find his owner, you and Jonathan are going to be roomies."

Lily nodded, resigned—for the moment. "Then I'd better get started trying to find his owner," she told Theresa.

With that, Lily retreated into the glass-enclosed cubbyhole where she came up with her recipes. It was a tiny office at best, with just enough space to fit an undersize desk and chair. She couldn't complain. It suited her needs. There was enough space on the desk for her laptop, which was all she required. That and the wireless portable printer she had set up on a folding table.

Lily got to work the second she sat down.

Deciding that an actual picture would do a better job than a drawing, she'd taken a picture of Jonathan earlier with the camera on her cell phone. After attaching her phone to the laptop, she proceeded to upload the photograph—adorable in her opinion—onto her laptop.

"Why would anyone not realize you were missing?" she murmured to the photograph. "Okay, enough of that, back to work," she ordered herself.

Centering the photograph and cropping it to focus on his face, she wrote in a few pertinent words about the puppy—where and when he was found—then put down her phone number.

Reviewing everything on the screen, Lily went ahead and printed one copy as a test run. Except for the fact that she needed to tweak the color a little to get it just right, the results looked fine to her. She adjusted the color and changed a couple of the words she'd initially used, then saved this copy over the first one. She printed a copy of this version.

She reviewed the poster one final time, decided she was satisfied with both the message and Jonathan's photograph and saved *this* version for posterity. Then she ran off an initial twenty-five posters. She intended to put them up on trees and poles throughout her entire residential development.

Hopefully, that would do it. If she received no response to the flyers, she'd be forced to widen her circle and take in the adjacent development, but for the moment, she was hoping that it wouldn't have to come to that.

If Jonathan *had* been her puppy, she'd be frantically searching for him by now. It only seemed right to her that his real owner would feel the same.

Once she and Jonathan left the catering shop for the day, Lily put her plan in motion. With the rear window cracked just far enough to let him have air, but not enough to allow the puppy to make an escape, she would drive from location to location within her development. She'd then get out—leaving the Labrador sitting in the backseat of her car—and put the flyers up on two to three trees.

Because she was trying to blanket the entire development, it took Lily more than an extra hour to get home. Jonathan barked louder and louder each time she got out, registering his growing displeasure at this game that seemed to be excluding him.

"You'll thank me when your owner turns up," Lily told the dog, getting in behind the wheel again. She had just tacked up the last of the posters.

Weary, she pulled up to her driveway. Jonathan began to bark again, as if anticipating that she was going to leave him behind.

"I'm coming," Lily assured him.

She rounded the hood of her vehicle to get to the rear passenger side. When she opened the rear door, she did her best to grab the leash the vet had given her but Jonathan was just too fast for her. He eluded her attempts and dove right between her legs as he made his break for freedom.

With a sigh, Lily gave up and let him go. She wasn't about to chase the animal down. With her luck, she'd fall flat on her face. Instead, she went to her trunk and unlocked it.

Theresa had insisted on making her a home-cooked meal—if home was a catering company—so that she'd have something substantial to eat for dinner.

"I know how you get all caught up in things and forget to eat, especially if you have to prepare something. Well, this time, you have no excuse," Theresa had told her as she thrust the large paper bag at her. The bottom had been warm to the touch.

It still was, Lily thought as she took the carefully packed, large paper bag out of the trunk.

Armed with her dinner, she walked up the drive-

way to the front door and then came perilously close
to dropping the bag.

Jonathan was sitting on her front step. By all appearances, the puppy looked as if he was waiting for her.

"What are you doing here?" she cried, stunned. "I
thought you'd be long gone by now."

Jonathan's expression was mournful as he glanced
up at her. His tongue was hanging out and he was
drooling onto her front step. The moment she inserted
her key into the lock, the Labrador shot to his feet. His
tail was thudding rhythmically on the step.

"I suppose you're going to want to come in," she
said. As if he understood her—or perhaps he just
wanted to be annoying, she speculated—Jonathan responded by barking at her. Barking even more loudly
than he had before. The sound made her absolutely
cringe as it echoed in her head. "House rule," she told
the puppy as she pushed the door open with her shoulder. Jonathan was inside the house like a shot. She had
to be careful not to trip on him—this was getting to be
a habit. The puppy seemed to be everywhere at once.
"Use your inside voice," she said firmly.

He chose to ignore her.

Jonathan barked again, just as loudly as before. Temporarily surrendering, Lily sighed as she closed the
door and then made her way into the kitchen.

"Maybe you don't have an inside voice. I'm beginning to think that you didn't run off, someone *dropped*
you off. Someone who didn't want to spend the rest of
their life living on headache medication."

Jonathan ran around her in a circle then, suddenly
and inexplicably, he apparently opted to become her

shadow. He started to follow her every move, staying within a couple of steps from her at all times.

"It's just going to be a matter of time before you make me fall, isn't it?" she predicted, putting down both the bag Theresa had prepared for her and the one Alfredo had given her earlier in the day. The chef had sent his assistant out to the pet store to buy some cans of dog food for Jonathan.

She might not have adopted the Labrador yet, but it seemed as if everyone else had, Lily thought as she unpacked the cans and set them on the counter. There were ten cans in all, each one for a different kind of meal.

"Boy, dogs eat better than most people, don't they?" she marveled. Jonathan was now running back and forth, eagerly anticipating being fed. "Can you smell this through the can?" she asked incredulously. Jonathan just continued pacing.

She took a moment to choose a can for her houseguest, decided that she couldn't make up her mind and finally made her selection by closing her eyes and plucking a can out of the group. One was as good as another, she reasoned. She had a feeling the puppy would have made short work of cardboard had she decided to serve him that.

The can conveniently had a pop-top. "At least I won't have to look for the can opener."

Lily pulled the top off and emptied the contents of the can into a soup bowl. Placing the bowl gingerly before the Labrador, she managed to take a couple of steps back, out of his way. That took a total of three seconds, possibly less.

Jonathan was finished eating in six.

Lily stared at the empty bowl. "Don't you even *chew?*" she asked in amazement. The puppy followed her when she picked up the bowl to wash it out. As before he seemed to be watching her every move intently. "If you think I'm going to give you any more food, you're going to be sadly disappointed. Your kitchen is closed for the night, mister. Water is all you're going to be getting until tomorrow."

Drying the bowl, she then filled it with cold water and placed it back on the floor where it had stood before. The dog taken care of, she turned to her own dinner. Lily opened up the containers of food that Theresa had sent home with her.

The woman had made her favorite, she realized. Beef stroganoff. One whiff of the aroma had her appetite waking up, reminding her that she hadn't eaten very much today.

"God bless Theresa," she murmured.

Putting together a serving, Lily sat down at the table. Jonathan placed himself directly by her feet. The Labrador watched every forkful of food she placed between her lips, seemingly mesmerized.

Lily did her very best to ignore the puppy and the soft brown eyes that were watching her so very closely. She held out against feeding Jonathan for as long as she could—nearly seven minutes—then finally capitulated with a heartfelt sigh.

"Here, finish it," she declared as she put her plate down on the floor.

She barely had enough time to pull her hand away. Even so, her thumb was almost a casualty. Jonathan's sharp little teeth just grazed the skin on her thumb as he proceeded to make the last of the stroganoff disappear from her plate.

"You know," she told the animal, "if we're going to get along for the duration of the time that you're here, we're going to need some boundaries. Boundaries that you're going to have to abide by or it's 'hit the street' for you, buddy. Am I making myself clear?" she asked the puppy.

Getting up from the table, she deposited the nearly immaculate plate in the sink and made her way to the family room. Her shadow followed. Jonathan's tongue was hanging out and he had started to drool again. This time he left an erratic, wet trail that led from the kitchen to the family room.

Turning around, Lily saw the newly forged trail. With a sigh, she took her sponge mop out of the closet and quickly went over the drool marks, cleaning them up. Finished, she left the mop leaning against the kitchen wall—confident she would need it again soon—and looked down at the puppy.

Now what? "Hey, Jonathan, are you up for a hot game of bridge?"

The puppy looked up at her and then began to bark. This time, the sound also rattled her teeth, not just her head.

"Didn't think so. Maybe I'll teach you the game someday." Her words played back to her. "Hey, what am I saying? You're not going to be here 'someday.' By the time 'someday' comes, you, my fine furry friend, will be long gone, eating someone else out of house and home and turning their home into a pile of rubble. Am I right?"

In response, Jonathan began to lick her toes.

She sank down on the sofa and began petting Jonathan's head. "You don't fight fair, Jonathan."

The puppy barked at her, as if to tell her that he already knew that.

Lily had a feeling it was going to be a very long night.

Chapter Five

Christopher glanced at his watch and frowned. It was five minutes later—four and a half, actually—since he'd last looked at it.

He was standing in the dog park, where he'd been standing for the past fifty minutes. From his vantage point, he had a clear view of the park's entrance. No one could enter—or leave—without his seeing it. It was another "typical day in paradise" as someone had once referred to the weather here in Bedford, the Southern California city where he'd grown up, but he wasn't thinking about the weather.

The frown had emerged, albeit slowly, because Lily and her Labrador puppy were now almost an hour late.

She didn't strike him as someone who would just not show up without at least calling, but then, he wasn't exactly the world's greatest judge of character, he reminded himself. Look how wrong he'd turned out to be about Irene.

He laughed shortly as the memory insisted on replaying itself in his mind. He would have bet money—and despite his outgoing nature, he didn't believe in gambling—that he and Irene were going to be together forever.

Idiot, he upbraided himself.

They'd met the first week at college. Helping each other acclimate to living away from home, they discovered that they had the same interests, the same goals—or so he'd thought. But while he went on to attend Cornell University to become a veterinarian, Irene's career path had her turning to the same New York University they'd gone to as undergraduates to get an advanced degree in investment banking.

The latter, he came to learn, was the career of choice in her family. She had her sights set on Wall Street. That was when their very serious first major conflict occurred. She wanted to remain in New York while he had always planned on eventually returning back "home" to set up his practice.

When he discovered that his mother was not only ill, but dying, he felt it was a sign that he really *needed* to return to Bedford. It was then that things between him and Irene began to unravel and he found that he really didn't know the woman the way he thought he did. Irene had made a halfhearted attempt to be understanding. She even said she was willing to take a short hiatus—she was already working at her father's firm—to accompany him to Bedford for one last visit to his mother.

The tension between them grew and he wound up

going back home to see his mother without her. Irene required "maintenance" and while that didn't bother him too often, he knew it would interfere with the time he wanted to sped with his mother.

As it was, that time turned out to be shorter than he'd anticipated. One month to the day after he had arrived back in Bedford, his mother lost her fight to stay alive. He was heartsick that she hadn't told him about her illness sooner, but grateful that at least he'd had those precious few weeks to spend with her.

When he returned to New York and Irene, things went from bad to worse. Their relationship continued to come apart. The night that he saw things clearly for the first time, Irene had told him that she wanted him to seriously consider turning his attention to doing something a little more "prestigious" than dealing with sickly animals.

She went on to say that in her opinion, as well as the opinions of her father and uncles, being a veterinarian didn't fit in with the upwardly mobile image that she was going for.

Irene had stunned him by handing him a list of "alternative careers" he could look into. "I kept hoping you'd come to this conclusion on your own, but if I have to prod you, I will. After all, what's a future wife for if not to get her man on the right path where he belongs?"

She'd actually meant that.

He knew then that "forever" had a very limited life expectancy in their particular case. He broke off the engagement as civilly as he could, being honest with Irene and telling her that much as he wanted to be with her, this wasn't the way he envisioned them spending their lives together: rubbing elbows with people more interested in profit than in doing some good.

Enraged, Irene had thrown her engagement ring at him. He left it where it fell, telling her she could keep it, that he didn't want it. Two days later, it showed up in his mailbox. He decided that he could always hock the diamond ring if he needed money for a piece of medical equipment.

He left New York for good the day after that.

In an incredibly short spate of time, he had lost his mother and the woman he had thought he loved.

It had taken him a while to get back into the swing of things. A while to stop thinking of himself as one half of a couple and to face life as a single person again. But then, he would remind himself when times were particularly tough emotionally, his mother had done it practically all of his life. His father, a policeman, had been off duty picking up a carton of milk at the local 7-Eleven when a desperate-looking gunman had rushed into the convenience store, waving his weapon around and demanding money. His father, according to the convenience store owner, tried to talk the gunman down.

The latter, jittery and, it turned out, high on drugs, shot him in the chest at point-blank range. The gunman got off three rounds before fleeing. He was caught less than a block away by the responding policemen. But they had arrived too late to save his father.

His mother had been devastated, but because he was only two years old at the time and they had no other family, she forced herself to rally, to give him as good a life as she could.

When he was about to go off to Cornell, he'd felt

guilty about leaving her alone. He remembered asking her why she'd never even dated anyone while he was growing up. She'd told him that she'd had one really great love in her life and she felt that it would have been greedy of her to try to get lightning to strike again.

"Your dad," she'd told him, "was a one-of-a-kind man and I was very lucky to have had him in my life, even for a little while. I don't want to spoil that by looking for someone to fill his shoes when I already know it can't be done."

However, he thought now with a smile, his mother would have told him that just because Irene hadn't turned out to be "the woman of his dreams," that didn't mean that there wasn't someone he was meant to be with out there, waiting for him to find her.

And then again, maybe not, he concluded with a sigh.

It wasn't that he was looking for a relationship. It was still too soon to be contemplating something like that. But nonetheless, he did find himself wanting to spend time with Lily.

Christopher looked at his watch again. Five more minutes had gone by.

Okay, he'd been at this long enough, he decided with a vague shrug. For whatever reason, Lily and her overenergetic puppy weren't coming and the woman hadn't seen fit to call him and let him know.

The possibility that the Lab's owner had turned up and claimed "Jonathan" did occur to him, but even in that event, Lily would have called to cancel, wouldn't she?

Unless, maybe, she'd lost his card.

You can stand here all day and come up with a

dozen excuses for her, but the fact is that she's not here and you are. It's time to go home, buddy, he silently ordered himself.

With that, Christopher straightened up away from the lamppost he'd been leaning against and began to head for where he had parked his car, a late-model, light gray four-door Toyota.

That was when he heard it.

A loud, high-pitched whistle literally seemed to *pierce* the air. It was an irritating sound, but he dismissed it—until he heard it again. His curiosity aroused, he looked around to see where the sound was coming from.

Before he could zero in on the source, a puppy was excitedly running circles around him.

The puppy.

There was a leash flying behind him like a light green streamer. For the moment, the puppy was a free canine.

With a laugh, Christopher stooped down to the puppy's level, petting him and ruffling the fur on his head. The animal responded like a long-lost friend who had finally made a connection with him against all odds.

"Hi, boy. Where's your mistress? Did you make a break for it?"

Christopher looked over his shoulder and this time he saw her. Lily. Her chestnut hair flying behind her, she was running toward him. Lily was wearing a striking green T-shirt that was molding itself to her upper torso and faded denim shorts, frayed at the cuff, which only seemed to accentuate her long legs.

Lily was covering a lot of ground, trying to catch

up to the dog that had obviously managed to get away from her.

Seeing that Jonathan had found the man they were both coming to meet, Lily slowed down just a tad, allowing herself time to catch her breath so that she could speak without gasping.

"Hi," Christopher greeted her warmly, the fifty-five-plus minutes he'd been waiting conveniently vanishing into an abyss. "I was beginning to think you weren't coming."

"I'm sorry about that," she apologized. "I'm usually very punctual." Since Christopher was still crouching next to the puppy, she dropped down to the ground beside him. It seemed easier to talk that way. "Jonathan decided he wanted to give me attitude instead of cooperation." She wasn't trying to get sympathy from the vet, she just wanted the man to know what had kept her from being here on time. "I had a terrible time getting him into the car. It was like he was just all paws, spread out in all directions. And then, when I finally got to the park and opened the rear door, he raced out of the car before I could get hold of his leash. I tried to grab it, but Jonathan was just too fast for me." She shook her head. "He obviously has a mind all his own."

It was hard to believe that the whirlwind of stubbornness she was describing was the same dog that now appeared to be all obliging sweetness and light. Not only that, but the Labrador had just flipped onto his back, paws resting in the begging position because he wanted to have his belly rubbed.

Christopher obliged. The puppy looked as if he was in heaven. "Was that you I heard, whistling just now?" Christopher asked her incredulously.

He was wording his question politely, she noted. Embarrassed, Lily nodded.

"I know the whistle was kind of loud." The truth of it was that she didn't know *how* to whistle quietly. "But I was desperate to get him to at least stop running away even if he wasn't coming back to me."

Christopher found it rather amusing that someone as petite and graceful as Lily whistled like a sailor on shore leave gathering his buddies together. But he decided that was an observation best kept to himself, at least for now. He had a feeling that if he mentioned his impression to her, Lily would take it as criticism and it would undoubtedly cause her to feel self-conscious around him. That was the *last* thing he wanted to do. If nothing else, it would get in the way of her being able to adequately relate to the puppy she was so obviously meant to bond with.

So instead, Christopher aimed his attention—as well as his words—at the black furry creature that all but had his head squarely in his lap, still silently begging for attention and to be petted.

This, Christopher decided, was a dog that thrived on positive reinforcement. That should ultimately make it easier for Lily.

"Have you been giving your mistress a hard time, Jonny-boy?" Christopher laughed, continuing to stroke the puppy. "Well, that's going to stop as of right now, do I make myself clear?" he asked in a pseudostern voice.

Eager-to-please brown eyes stared up at him, and then Jonathan's pink tongue darted out to quickly lick his hand. The same hand that had just been petting the animal.

Christopher pulled his hand out of the dog's reach.

"No more of that for a while. You're not fooling anyone. We're here to work," he told the dog as he got up off the ground. The next moment, the leash in one hand, he offered his other hand to Lily. "C'mon, it's time to start both your training lessons."

Taking his hand, Lily had the momentary sensation of being enveloped and taken care of. The man had strong hands. He also wasn't as quick to let her hand go as she would have thought. It was just an extra second or so, but it registered.

Feeling herself start to flush, Lily quickly changed the subject. "You made it sound as if you're going to be training me, as well," she said with a nervous laugh.

The laugh dissipated in her throat when he looked at her with a wide smile and replied good-naturedly, "That's because I am."

Lily was so stunned by his answer that for a couple of minutes, she had no reply to render, snappy or otherwise. And then her brain finally kicked in.

"I'm happy to say that I'm housebroken," she told Christopher.

She watched, nearly mesmerized, as the corners of his mouth slowly curved. She found herself being drawn into his smile. The line "resistance is futile" flashed through her brain.

"Good to know," Christopher told her, "but that isn't exactly what I have in mind for you."

"Oh?"

She looked at him warily, unaccountably relieved that they were out in the open, in a fairly crowded area. For the life of her, she wouldn't have been able to explain why the thought of being alone with the man made her fingertips tingle and the rest of her feel nervous. She did her best not to let him see the effect he was having on her.

"And what is it that you have in mind for me?" she asked, brazening it out. It was a loaded question and had they been friends for some length of time, or at least at a stage where they knew one another a little better, the answer that flashed through her brain might have been obvious.

"I intend to train you on how to train Jonny here," he told Lily. "There's a right way and a wrong way to do just about everything. With a dog, the wrong way won't get you the results you want and it could get you in trouble. Remember, it's important to maintain positive reinforcement. I don't care if it's a treat—a small one," he emphasized, warning, "or you'll wind up with a severely overweight dog—or lavish praise, as long as it's positive. Remember, kindness works far better than fear," he told her as they began to walk to the heart of the park.

"Fear?" she repeated uncertainly. The word conjured up vivid memories of her own reaction to Jonathan and his nipping teeth.

Christopher nodded. "I've seen people scream at their pets, hit them with a rolled-up newspaper or anything else that happened to be handy. The pet was always the worse for it. You don't want your pet to be obedient out of fear but out of love. I can't stress that enough," he told her. And then he curtailed the rest of his lecture, as if not wanting to get carried away. "Although I have to admit that you don't look like the type who would take a stick to a dog."

Lily shivered at the very thought of someone actually beating their pet. Why would anyone get a pet if they had no patience? Every relationship, whether strictly involving humans, or extending to pets, required a large dose of patience unless it happened to be unfolding on the big screen in the guise of a popular studio's full-length cartoon feature.

"Also," he continued as they made their way to a more open section of the park, "regarding housebreaking—there will be occasional setbacks," he warned her. "I don't recommend dragging Jonny back and sticking his nose into what just came out his other end while sternly denouncing him, saying, 'No, no!' Best-case scenario," Christopher explained patiently, "all that teaches him is to do it somewhere a little more out of the way so he won't get reprimanded for it."

"And worst-case scenario?" she asked, curious what he thought that was since what he'd just described *was* worst-case scenario as far as she was concerned.

Christopher laughed softly. "Your puppy just might find he has a taste for it. I've heard of more than one dog who believed in recycling his or her own waste products." He stopped walking, taking a closer look at Lily's face. "You look a little pale," he noted. "Are you all right?"

She put her hand over her stomach, as if that would keep her hastily consumed breakfast from rising up in her throat and purging itself from her stomach. Opening her door to this puppy had consequently left her open to more things than she'd ever dreamed of, no pun intended she added silently.

"I just didn't realize all the things that were involved in taking in a stray—even temporarily. The only dogs I ever knew were up on a movie screen," she confessed. Admittedly it had been a very antiseptic way of obtaining her knowledge. "They didn't smell, didn't go to the bathroom and had an IQ just a tad lower than Einstein's." She smiled ruefully as she elaborated a little more, realizing while she was at it that she was underscoring her naïveté. "The kind that when their owner said, 'I need a screw driver' would wait until he specified whether it was a flathead or Phillips head that he wanted."

Christopher grinned. He liked that she could laugh at herself. The fact that Lily had a sense of humor was a very good sign, as far as he was concerned.

"In the real world, if you don't bathe them, dogs smell, and they don't do long division in their heads." And then he went on to list just a few of the positive reasons to own a dog. "But they *do* respond to the sound of your voice, are highly trainable and will come to an understanding with you, given the time and the training—coupled with a lot of patience. Always remember, anything worth doing is worth doing well. You let a dog into your life, remember to show him that while you love him, you're the one in charge, and you will never regret it."

Christopher paused for a moment. He caught himself looking into her eyes and thinking how easily he could get lost in them if he wasn't careful.

Taking a breath, he told himself that he needed to get down to business before she got the wrong idea about him and why he was here.

"Now then, are you ready to get started?" he asked Lily.

"Ready," she answered with a smart nod, eager to begin.

"All right," he said, stooping down to the dog's level

again to remove the leash he'd given her. He replaced it with a long line, a leash that was three times as long as the initial one. Getting back up to his feet, Christopher told her, "The first thing we want to teach Jonny here is to come when you call."

She watched as he slowly backed up, away from Jonathan. "Um, how about housebreaking?" she asked hesitantly.

She would have thought that would be the very first thing the dog would be taught. She'd had to clean up several rather untidy messes already and couldn't see herself doing that indefinitely. To be honest, she'd rather hoped that the vet had some sort of magic solution regarding housebreaking that he was willing to pass on to her.

The sympathetic expression on his handsome, chiseled face told her that she'd thought wrong.

"That's going to take a little longer for him to learn, I'm afraid. I can—and will—show you the basics and what to say, but for the most part, that's going to require dedication and patience on your part. A *lot* of dedication and patience," he emphasized. "Because you're going to have to take Jonny here out every hour on the hour until he goes—as well as watch for signs that he's about to go."

This was completely new territory for her and something she had never given any attention to before now. "How will I know what signs to look for?"

"That," he replied with a smile that would have curled her toes had she allowed it, "is a very good question." Leaning in to her as if to confide a secret, he lowered his voice and said, "This would be the part where *you* get trained."

Drawing his head back again, he gave her a wink that seemed to flutter through layers of skin tissue and embed itself smack in the middle of her stomach.

"Okay, back to getting him to come when you call," he said, taking a firm hold on the long line. With that, he proceeded to go through the basics for her slowly and clearly before he went on to demonstrate what he'd just said, allowing her to see it in action.

Chapter Six

"Okay, now you try," Christopher said after success-fully getting Jonathan to come to him when he called the puppy. The vet held out the long line to her.

Instead of taking it from him, Lily looked at the elongated leash uncomfortably. "Me?"

If there was one thing she really hated, it was ap-pearing inept in front of people, even someone who seemed as nice as this man. Doing so only seemed to underscore her feelings of insecurity, not to mention that it reinforced the shyness that she grappled with every day.

Christopher instinctively knew when a situation re-quired an extra dose of patience. Usually, it involved the animals he treated, but occasionally, he could sense the need to tap into his almost endless supply when dealing with a person. He could see that Lily's reluctance had nothing to do with being stubborn or reticent. From her stance, she was far from confident.

That had to change. If he could sense it, the dog definitely could. While he had a soft spot in his heart for all things canine, he also knew that dominance had to be established. If it wasn't, this cute little black ball of fur and paws was going to walk all over the woman beside him and most likely make her life a living hell— or at least turn her home into a shambles.

"Well, yes," Christopher told her. "Unless you intend to have me come home with you and take over raising Jonny here, you're going to have to learn how to make him obey you. Emphasis on the word *obey*," he said, still holding the end of the long line before her.

Lily pressed her lips together. The only thing she hated more than looking like a fool was looking like a coward. She took a deep breath and wrapped her fingers around the end of the long line.

Glaring at the puppy, she said as authoritatively as she could, "Come!" When Jonathan remained where he was, she repeated the command even more forcefully. "Come!" At which point Jonathan cocked his head and stared at her, but made no attempt to comply.

Taking pity on her, Christopher bent close to her ear and said in a low voice, "Remember to preface each command with his name and give the long line a little tug the way I did. He'll get the hang of it eventually."

Christopher's breath along the side of her face and neck would have caused an involuntary shiver to shimmy down her spine had she not steeled herself at the last moment.

Lily felt her cheeks growing pink. Use the puppy's

name. How could she have forgotten something so simple so quickly?

"Right. Jonathan, come!" she ordered, simultaneously giving the elongated leash a little tug.

Despite its length, the impact of the play on the line telegraphed itself to the Labrador. Then, to her surprised relief, Jonathan trotted toward her, coming to a halt almost on top of her feet.

"He did it," she cried excitedly, stunned and thrilled at the same time. "He came!"

Christopher wasn't sure which was more heartening to him, seeing the animal respond to Lily's command or seeing Lily's joy *because* the animal had responded to her command.

"Yes, he did," Christopher acknowledged with a pleased smile. "Now give him that scrap of doggie sausage as a reward and play out the long line so you can do it again."

Jonathan appeared to be in sheer ecstasy as he swallowed his "reward" without so much as pausing a second to chew it.

It was a toss-up as to which appeared to be more eager for a repeat of what had just happened, Christopher mused: Jonathan or his mistress.

The brief exercise played out more smoothly this time.

"Again," Christopher instructed her after Lily tossed the treat to the eager puppy.

Lily and Jonathan repeated the training exercise a total of five times before Christopher decided it was time to move on to the next command.

"This is the exact opposite of what you've just taught him," Christopher told her. He noticed that instead of

the reluctance she had initially exhibited, Lily seemed
to be almost as eager as the puppy to undertake the
next "lesson." "You're going to train him to stay where
he is. Now, not moving might seem like it's an easy
thing to get across, but for an antsy puppy that's approximately six to seven weeks old, staying put is not
part of their normal behavior—unless they're asleep,"
he told her. "Okay, instead of tugging on the long line,
you're going to use a hand gesture—holding your hand
out to him as if you were a cop stopping traffic—plus
a calm voice and patience. Lots of patience," Christopher emphasized.

"Okay," she said, nodding her head.

In a way, he couldn't help thinking that she reminded him of the puppy—all eagerness and enthusiasm. Without fully realizing it, she'd gone a step up in
his estimation of her.

"You tell him to stay and then slowly back away
from him," Christopher instructed, standing directly
behind her and ready to match her step for step as
she backed up. "Until he responds for the first time
and stays in place for as long as you've designated,
you don't take your eyes off him. *Make* him obey
you. Your goal ultimately is to get Jonny to obey the
sound of your voice *without* being bribed to do it or
being watched intently. And that," he told her firmly,
"is going to take doing the same thing over and over
again until he gets it, until he associates what he does
with the key words you use."

"I was never very good at being authoritative," Lily
admitted ruefully. But even so, her enthusiasm was
still high.

"Then you're going to have to keep that little secret

to yourself. As far as Jonny here is concerned, you are the lord and master of his world—or mistress of it if you prefer," he amended.

She didn't seem like the type to take offense over words where none was intended, Christopher thought, but since they were still in the getting-to-know-each-other stage, he wasn't about to take anything for granted.

Lily smiled at him. There was something about the way she looked at him that made him feel connected to her. It was as if, without his exactly knowing why, they were in sync to one another. "Either way is fine with me," she told him.

In all honesty, she'd never thought of herself in those sort of lofty terms. She was neither a mistress *nor* a master. Or at least she hadn't been until now, she thought with a smile.

"Okay." Christopher nodded toward their subject. "Let's see you make him stay."

"You're not going to do it first?" she asked Christopher.

"You mean warm him up for you?" he asked, amused. "He's your dog," he told her, wanting to subtly build up her confidence. "You should be the main authority figure he listens to."

"But he's not my dog," she protested. "I have these flyers out in my development. His owner might still come looking for him." Although, she had to admit, she was now just a tad less eager for that to happen than she had been just a little while ago.

He looked at Lily for a long moment, seeing through the veneer she'd put up. "Then tell me again why you're going to all this trouble for an animal you might not get to keep?"

There was a struggle going on inside of her, a struggle between logic and emotions. At any given moment, she wasn't quite sure just which way she was leaning.

But for the sake of appearances and the role she was trying to maintain, Lily replied, "I'm trying to train Jonathan so that I can survive with him until his owner *does* turn up." She did her best to sound cool and removed as she added, "I don't want to get attached to him and then have to give him up."

"I hate to break this to you, Lily, but watching the two of you, in my opinion, you already *are* attached to him—and it looks to me as if he's attached to you as well, as much as an overenergized puppy can be attached to one person," he qualified with a laugh. "Don't get me wrong," he was quick to explain. "Dogs are extremely loyal creatures, but puppies tend to sell their souls for a belly rub and have been known to walk off with almost anyone—unless they've been given a better reason to stay where they are."

Christopher searched her eyes. He could readily see that Lily was grappling with the problem of wanting to keep the dog at an arm's length emotionally—while wanting to throw caution to the wind and enjoy the unconditional love that the puppy offered.

"And if I could add two more cents." Christopher paused, waiting for her to nod her head.

Surprised, she told him, "Go ahead."

"Personally, I don't think anyone is going to come looking for Jonny here," he told her. "The way I see it, his mom probably had a litter recently and this one made a break for it when he was old enough to explore the world and no one was watching him. Most likely, his mom's owner was busy trying to find a good home for him and his brothers and sisters. When Jonny took off, the owner probably took it to be a blessing—one less puppy for him to place.

"*Or* he might have been so overwhelmed that he didn't even notice Jonny was missing—especially if his dog had had an unusually large litter." A fond smile curved his lips as he gazed down at the Labrador that had taken to momentarily sunning himself and was stretched out in the grass. "These little guys move around so fast, it's hard to get a proper head count."

She couldn't quite explain the happy feeling growing inside of her, especially since she was trying so hard to maintain her barriers, so hard to not get attached and thereby leave herself open to another onslaught of pain.

Attempting to sound removed—and not quite succeeding—she said, "So what you're telling me is that I'd better get used to the idea of vacuuming up fur several times a week."

For the sake of her charade, Christopher inclined his head—even though he saw right through her performance. "That's another way of putting it."

She was on shaky ground and she had a feeling that she wasn't fooling him—or herself. "What if I don't like the idea of having to vacuum that often?" she posed.

Rather than tell her that he would take the dog—which he actually would do if he believed she was serious—Christopher decided to play on her sympathies and create a heart-tugging scenario.

"Well, in that case, you could always bring Jonny

to the animal shelter and leave him there. Bedford outlawed euthanizing animals after a certain period of time the way they do in some other cities, so there's no chance of his being put to sleep. Of course, he might not get all the love and attention he needs, getting lost in the shuffle because there are a large number of animals at the shelter. The city had to cut back on employees even though the animals all need care and attention.

"Not to mention the fact that lately the number of volunteers who come by to walk, feed and play with the animals has dropped off, too, but at least the little guy would still be alive—just not as happy as he would be here with you."

Beneath the steel exterior she was trying to maintain was a heart made of marshmallow. But even if there wasn't, Lily would have seen what the veterinarian was trying to do.

Shaking her head, she told him, "You left out the violins."

The comment, seemingly coming out of the blue, caught him by surprise. "What?"

"Violins," she repeated, then elaborated. "As background music. You left them out. They should have been playing while you painted that scene for me. They could have swelled to a crescendo right toward the end. But other than that, you just created a scenario that's bordering on being a tearjerker."

"Just wanted you to know what these little critters are up against," he told her with a very straight face. "Now, let's see if you can get Jonny to stay. In place," he added with emphasis in case she thought he was still referring to the dog staying with her. And then he winked at her.

Again.

Her reaction was exactly the same as it had been the first time he'd winked at her. Her breath caught in her throat and butterflies fluttered in her stomach. The only difference was that it seemed to her that there were even more now than there had been the first time he'd winked at her.

How could something that could technically be described as a twitch create such pure havoc inside of her? Was she really *that* starved for attention that any hint of it had her practically melting into tiny little puddles and reminding herself to breathe?

Lily had no idea how to begin to make any sense of that.

For the moment, she blocked it all out and turned her attention to what Christopher had just said, not how she'd reacted to how he'd looked as he said it.

"Okay, let's see if I can get him to listen."

"Oh, he'll listen," Christopher assured her. "That's not the issue. Whether he'll obey is a totally other story."

This particular story turned out to have a good ending some ninety minutes later.

With Christopher urging her on, she had managed to get the Labrador puppy to stay in place for a total of ten seconds as she backed away from him. This happened several times, building up her confidence both in herself and in her relationship with the eager Labrador. She'd still had to maintain eye contact with Jonathan, but Christopher promised her that that would change and the next time they got together, they'd work on her just turning her back on the Labrador and *still* getting the animal to remain in place.

"Next time?" Lily repeated. It wasn't exactly a question so much as she wanted to make sure that she'd heard him correctly.

"Yes, next weekend," Christopher answered.

He slanted a glance at her, wondering if he'd pushed a little too hard too fast. Normally, he wouldn't have given it a second thought, but this woman needed a little more delicate care in his estimation. He also felt certain she was worth it. Something about her aroused both his protective nature as well as an inherent response from him as a man. Though a little soured on the idea of relationships, he still genuinely *liked* this woman.

"I thought since you were having such success at this, you might want to push on, get a few more commands under your belt, so to speak. Unless you don't want to," Christopher said, giving her a way out if she really wanted one.

"Oh, I want to." She'd said that a little too eagerly, Lily realized and dialed back her enthusiasm a notch as she continued. "But what I'm really interested in is getting him housebroken," she confessed, wondering if she was putting the veterinarian out too much, taking advantage of his generosity.

"For that to get underway, we can't be out here," he told her. "We'd have to work with him at your home. Jonny can't be taught to observe his boundaries if one of those boundaries is missing," he pointed out.

"Can't argue with that," she agreed. And then she glanced at her watch.

Christopher saw something that resembled an apologetic expression on her face. Had he missed something? "What's the matter?"

"I feel guilty that you're spending all this time helping me train Jonathan when you could be doing something else with your time. I wouldn't feel so bad if you were letting me pay you for your time, but you're not."

"I'm not about to charge you for something I volunteered to do." He could see that wasn't going to assuage her guilt. He thought of the other day—and went with that. "However, if you feel compelled to make some more pastries anytime soon, well, I couldn't very well refuse those, now could I?"

"How about dinner?" She was as surprised as he was to hear her make the suggestion. It seemed to have come out all on its own. For a second, she lapsed into stunned silence.

The sentence was just hanging there between them, so he took a guess at what she was saying. "You mean like going out to dinner first?"

You put it out there, now follow up on it before the man thinks he's spending time with a crazy woman.

"No, I mean how about if I make you dinner before the dessert? Like a package deal," she concluded with a bright, albeit somewhat nervous smile.

For just a heartbeat, he found himself mesmerized by her smile. Some people had smiles that seemed to radiate sunshine and make a person feel the better for being in its presence. Lily had such a smile.

"I wouldn't want you to go to all that trouble," he finally said when he recovered his ability to make coherent sentences. But he uttered it without very much conviction.

"Not that it's any actual trouble," she countered,

"but why not? It seems to me like you're going through a lot of trouble helping me train Jonathan."

There were two people running around the perimeter of the park with their whippets. Moving out of their way, Christopher waited until they were out of earshot before continuing their verbal dueling match.

"I don't consider working with a dog as any sort of 'trouble.' To be honest, I can't remember a time when I didn't want to be a veterinarian," he told her. "My dad died when I was very young and my mother thought that having a dog—or two—around the house would somehow help fill the void in my life that his death left. Without knowing it, she inadvertently set me on a career path that shaped the rest of my life. I really appreciated what she tried to do, but to be honest, you can't miss what you don't remember ever having, can you?"

"Actually, you *could* miss it if you find yourself imagining what it would have been like to have a father and then realize that no matter what you do, it was never going to be that way."

There was a sadness in her voice that caught his attention. "You sound like someone who's had firsthand experience with that."

Ordinarily, she would have just glossed over his observation, shrugging it off and simply saying no, she didn't. But lying—which was what it amounted to from her point of view—just didn't seem to be right in this situation. Even a little white one would have troubled her.

"I do," she admitted. For a moment, as she brought her childhood into focus, she avoided his eyes. "I never knew my dad. He took off before I was born. The story went that he told my mother he wasn't cut out to be a father and that then he proved it by just taking off," she concluded with a shrug that was way too careless to be what it portrayed.

He wanted to put his arms around her, to not just comfort her but to silently offer her protection against the world, as well. Until this moment, those reactions in him had been strictly confined to dealing with creatures in the animal kingdom. This was a whole new turn of events. But even so, he kept his hands at his sides, sensing that he might just scare her off if he did something so personal so early in their acquaintance.

So he restricted his response to a verbal one. "I'm sorry."

"Yes, I was, too—for my mother." Her father had abandoned the person she had loved the most in life— her mother. And for that, she could never forgive the man. "She could have used a little help juggling raising me and paying the bills. Life was a constant struggle for her."

"That's the way I felt, too," he admitted. "But my mother never complained. I don't think I *ever* heard her even say a cross word against anyone. She just plowed through life, doing what she had to do."

"Mine held down two jobs trying to do the same thing." It felt almost eerie the way their lives seemed to mirror each other when it came to family life. She didn't normally seek details, but she did this time. "You have any siblings?"

Christopher shook his head. It was the one area that he wished had been different. "None. You?"

"Same," she answered. "None."

It should have felt eerie to her—but it didn't. Instead, she realized that it made her feel closer to this outgoing man. She knew the danger in that, but for now, she just allowed it to be, taking comfort in the warm feeling that was being generated inside of her.

Chapter Seven

He walked Lily to her car, which was parked not that far from his own.

As he stood to the side and waited for her to coax the Labrador into the backseat, Christopher realized that he wasn't quite ready for their afternoon to come to an end.

His reaction surprised him. He hadn't felt any real interest in maintaining any sort of female companionship since his less-than-amicable breakup with Irene a few months ago. Maybe he was finally ready to move on with his life in every sense.

Watching Lily now, Christopher decided he had nothing to lose by suggesting that perhaps they could just continue with Jonathan's training session in a different setting.

As she turned away from the dog and closed the

rear passenger door, Christopher pretended to glance at his watch.

Looking up again, he said to her, "Listen, I have nothing scheduled for the rest of the day. Why don't I just follow you to your place and we'll get a head start in housebreaking your houseguest?"

"Really?"

"Really," Christopher answered. He didn't, however, want her having any unrealistic expectations about what they were going to accomplish this afternoon. "Remember, though, I did say 'get a head start.' This isn't a relatively quick process, like getting Jonny to come or stay. Or even getting him to do something trickier like rolling over or sitting up and begging. This," he warned her, "is going to take a while. With some luck and a lot of vigilance, best-case scenario, you might be able to get him completely housebroken in two weeks."

"But I work and the hours aren't always regular," she told Christopher. Looking at Jonathan in the backseat, she lamented, "How can I keep up a regular schedule with him?"

"That is a problem," Christopher conceded. "But it's not impossible."

She found herself clinging to those words like a drowning woman to a life preserver. If she was going to wind up actually keeping Jonathan, she would be eternally grateful that Theresa had sent her to this veterinarian. He was a godsend.

"Okay, I'm listening."

"You take him out every hour on the hour when you *are* home. When you're not, you can leave him in a puppy crate."

"A puppy crate?" she repeated, not knowing if she was just stunned or actually horrified by the suggestion. She had to have misunderstood him. "You're telling me to stick Jonathan in a crate?" she asked in disbelief. "That's cruel."

"No, actually, it's not cruel at all. Puppy crates come in different sizes to accommodate the different breeds. They're airy and specifically designed to make the puppy feel safe. Puppies are placed in puppy crates for the same reason that they tightly bundle up newborn babies in a hospital. They actually like small spaces. An added bonus is if they only spend part of their time there each day—such as when you're away at work— they won't mess the crate up because they won't go to the bathroom where they sleep."

"What about in the pet stores?" she countered. She'd seen more than one employee in a pet store having to clean out the cages that the animals were kept in.

"That's because the animals are kept in their cages all the time. They have no choice but to relieve themselves in the same place that they sleep. Those conditions make it harder to train an animal, but not in the case I'm suggesting," he pointed out.

She could tell by his tone when he described conditions in a pet store that the veterinarian didn't really approve of them. Still, the idea of forcing Jonathan to spend part of his time in a crate didn't exactly sit well with her.

"Not that I'm doubting what you just said about puppy crates, but isn't there any other way to house-break him? I really don't like the idea of sticking Jonathan in a cage—or crate—unless I have no other choice." She looked at the dog, sympathy welling up inside of her. "It just seems too much like making him spend time in prison to me," she confessed.

He liked the fact that despite her attempts at projecting bravado, Lily was a pushover when it came to animals. "Well, there is one other alternative," he told her.

Lily second-guessed him. "Taking him to work with me, the way I did the first day."

"Or you could drop him off at my animal hospital when you go to work and then I could drop him off with you in the evening. Unless you were leaving earlier than I was, and then you could just come and get Jonny. And in between, I can have one of the animal techs make sure our boy here doesn't have any embarrassing 'accidents.'"

That really sounded as if it was the far better choice in her opinion, but again, she felt as if it would definitely be putting him out.

"Wouldn't they mind?" she asked, adding, "Wouldn't *you* mind?"

"No and no," Christopher answered. He leaned against the side of her vehicle as he laid out his new plan for her. "I passed around those pastries you dropped off the other day and if you're willing to supply the staff with them, say once a week or so, I *know* that they'd be more than happy to pitch in and get Jonny here potty trained," he guaranteed.

Since they were still talking, he opened the front passenger door to allow air to circulate through the vehicle for the Labrador. At the same time, he placed his body in the way so that the puppy couldn't come bounding out and escape.

"You're serious?" Lily asked.

She could feel herself growing hopeful again. This

last idea was infinitely appealing—and it meant she wouldn't have to feel guilty about putting the puppy into a cage just to keep her house from turning into one giant puppy latrine.

"Completely," Christopher replied with no reservations.

"Then it's a deal," she declared.

"Great. I'll alert the staff to start looking for new clothes one size larger than they're wearing right now," he said with a straight face. Only his eyes gave him away.

"You don't have to do that," Lily told him, waving away the suggestion.

To which he asked, "You've changed your mind about baking?"

There was no way that was about to happen. She absolutely loved baking, especially for an appreciative audience.

"Oh, no, it's not that," she said, dismissing his suggestion. "But I can duplicate the recipe and make a low-fat version—they'll never notice the difference—and nobody will need bigger clothing."

He appreciated what she was trying to do, but in his opinion, "lighter" was never "better." For that matter, it wasn't even as good as what it was supposed to be substituting.

"You say that now, but I can always tell the 'light' version of anything," he told her. "It never tastes the same."

Lily studied him for a long moment. Her expression was unreadable. And then he saw humor overtaking the corners of her mouth, curving it. "Are you challenging me?"

Christopher took measure of her. She meant well, but as an opponent, she was a lightweight.

"Not in so many words but, well, yes, maybe I am," he conceded.

Lily squared her shoulders. For the first time since she had come into his animal hospital, she looked formidable. It surprised him.

"Okay," Lily said with a nod of her head, "you're on. I'll bake my usual way, and then arbitrarily I'll make a batch of substitutes, and I defy you to definitively say which is which."

"You have a deal," he readily agreed, confident he'd win. He took her hand and shook it.

It was done as a matter of course, without any sort of separate, independent thought devoted to it. But the moment his strong fingers enveloped hers, she could have sworn she felt some sort of current registering, a shot akin to electricity suddenly coursing through her veins from the point of contact.

Her breath caught in her throat for the second time that day.

Out of nowhere, she suddenly caught herself wondering if he was going to kiss her.

The next second, she hastily dismissed the thought, silently asking herself if she was crazy. People didn't kiss after making what amounted to day boarding arrangements for their pet. That wasn't how these situations played themselves out.

Was it?

Clearing her throat, as if that somehow helped her shake off the thoughts swarming through her brain and turning up her body temperature to an almost alarming degree, Lily dropped the veterinarian's hand. She took a step back. She would have taken a few more, but her car was at her back, blocking any further retreat on her part.

"Do you still want to come over?" she heard herself asking in an almost stilted voice. "To start housebreaking him?"

Her mouth had gone completely dry by the end of the sentence.

"Unless you've changed your mind," Christopher qualified. He'd felt it, too, felt the crackle of electricity between them, felt a sudden longing in its wake that had left him a little shaken and unsteady. He was definitely attracted to this woman, but it was more than that. Just what, he wasn't sure.

Yet.

"No, I haven't," Lily heard herself saying.

Her own voice echoed in her head as if it belonged to someone else. Part of her, the part that feared what might be ahead of her, wanted to run and hide, to quickly thank him for his trouble and then jump into her car in order to make a hasty retreat.

But again, that would be the coward's way out.

What was she afraid of? Lily demanded silently. She was a grown woman who had been on her own for a while now, a grown woman who knew how to take care of herself. There was no one else to step up, no one else to take up her cause or fight any of her battles for her, so she had to stick up for herself. She was all she had to rely on and so far, she'd managed just fine—with a little help from Theresa.

Making up her mind, she decided that yes, she did want him to come over. She wanted his help—and if anything else developed along the way, well, she'd face it then and handle it.

"Let me give you my address in case we get separated," Lily said to him, taking a very small notepad out of her purse. Finding a pen took a couple of minutes longer, but she did and then she began to write down her address.

"Separated?" he questioned. "How fast do you intend to be driving?" he couldn't help asking.

"Not that fast," Lily assured him. "But there are always traffic lights turning red at the most inopportune time, impeding progress. I might make it through a light, but you might not, that sort of thing." Finished, she handed the small piece of paper to him. "Can you read it?" she asked. "My handwriting is pretty awful."

He looked down at the paper—and laughed. "You think this is bad? You should see the way some of my friends write—it's enough to make a pharmacist weep," Christopher told her with another laugh.

Glancing one last time at the address she'd written down for him, he folded the paper and put it in his pocket. "Just let me get to my car before you start yours," he told her. "I'll take it from there."

"Okay," Lily answered gamely.

She rounded the back of the vehicle—Jonathan eyeing her every move—and got in behind the steering wheel. Buckling up, she not only remained where she was until Christopher got to his car but waited until he started the vehicle and pulled out of the row where he had been parked, as well.

Only then did she turn her key in the ignition, back out and head for the exit. Within less than a minute, she was on the thoroughfare leading away from the dog park.

Lily glanced in her rearview mirror to make sure that Christopher was following her.

He was.

Meanwhile, Jonathan had taken to pacing back and forth on the seat behind her as she drove them home. Each time she came to a stop at an intersection light, even when she rolled into that stop, Jonathan would suddenly and dramatically pitch forward.

After emitting a high-pitched yelp that sounded like it could have easily doubled for a cry for help, the puppy apparently decided it was safer for him to lie low, which he did. He spread himself out as far as he could on the backseat and seemed to all but make himself one with the cushion.

"It's not far now," Lily promised the Labrador, hoping that if he didn't understand the words, at least the sound of her calm voice would somehow help soothe him.

If it did—and she had her suspicions that it might have because he'd stopped making those strange, whiny noises—the effect only lasted until she pulled up in her driveway some fifteen minutes later.

The second she put the vehicle into Park and got out, Jonathan was up on all fours again, pacing along the backseat—when he wasn't sliding down because of a misstep that sent his paws to the floor.

Since she had kept the windows in the back partially open, she didn't immediately open the rear door to let him out. Instead, she waited for Christopher to pull up alongside of her vehicle. She felt that he could handle the Labrador far better than she could. For one thing, the man was a lot stronger.

The minutes began to slip away, banding together to form a significant block of time.

When Christopher still didn't show up, she began to wonder if he had somehow lost sight of her. She'd stopped looking in the rearview mirror around the time when Jonathan's head was in her direct line of vision, blocking out everything else.

And then she realized that it didn't really matter if Christopher had lost sight of her car or not. She'd given him her address, so even if he had lost sight of her vehicle he still should have been pulling up in her driveway by now.

Since he wasn't, she took it as a sign that he'd changed his mind about coming over.

The more the minutes ticked away, the more certain she became that she was right. Somewhere along the route, he had obviously decided that he had given her enough of his time.

She felt a strange sensation in her stomach, as if it was puckering and twisting.

Why his sudden change of heart left her feeling let down, she didn't know. After all, it wasn't as if this was a date or anything. The man had already been extremely helpful, getting her started on the proper way to train her dog, and she was very grateful for that. No reason to be greedy, Lily silently insisted. The man had already gone over and above the call of duty.

Jonathan began to whine, bringing her back to her driveway and the immediate situation. She was allowing her disappointment to hijack her common sense.

Lily quickly shut down any stray emotions that threatened to overwhelm her.

"Sorry," she apologized to the puppy. She opened the rear passenger door a crack—just wide enough to allow her to grab his leash. She was learning. "I didn't mean to forget about you," she told the dog.

Getting a firm hold of the leash, Lily opened the door all the way.

Jonathan needed no further encouragement. He came bounding out, savoring his freedom like a newly released prisoner after a lengthy incarceration.

"Easy," she cautioned. "Easy now!"

The words had absolutely no effect on Jonathan, a fact that only managed to frustrate her. And then she remembered what Christopher had taught the dog— and relatedly, what he had taught her.

Grabbing a firmer hold on the leash, she said in the most authoritative-sounding voice she could summon, "Jonathan, stay!"

The dog abruptly stopped trotting toward the house and stood as still as a statue, waiting for her to "release" him from her verbal hold with the single word Christopher had told her to use.

Getting her bearings, Lily turned toward the front of the house so that the dog wouldn't catch her off guard when he resumed running. Only then did she say, "Okay," in the same authoritative voice.

Just as she'd expected, the very next moment Jonathan was back to bounding toward the front door.

Lily was right on his heels. "Someday, dog, you are just going to have to get a grip on that enthusiasm of yours. But I guess that day isn't going to be today," she said, resigned to having a barely harnessed tiger by the tail—at least for a few more weeks.

The veterinarian's idea of having her drop the dog off at his animal hospital each morning was beginning to sound better and better, she thought as she unlocked her front door.

Once Jonathan had passed over the threshold, she let the leash go and entered the house herself. She locked her front door a moment later. There had been several break-ins in the development in the past couple of months and she was determined that her house was not going to be part of those statistics.

Turning from the door, Lily looked down at the dog. "Looks like we're on our own tonight, Jonathan. But that's okay, we don't need Christopher around. We'll do just fine without him."

The dog whined in response.

Lily sighed, sinking down on the couch. "I know, I know, who am I kidding? We're not really fine on our own, but we just have to make the best of it, right? Glad to hear you agree," she told the dog, pretending to take his silence as agreement.

She thought of the housebreaking lessons that lay ahead of her. No time like the present, right?

"What do you say to having some superearly dinner. We'll fill that tummy of yours and then spend the rest of the evening trying to empty it. Sound like fun to you?" she asked, looking at the puppy. "Me, neither," she agreed. "But what has to be done, has to be done, so we might as well get started. The sooner this sinks in for you, the happier both of us are going to be."

Just then, she heard her cell phone ringing. Her first thought was that Theresa had gotten another booking and wanted to run a few desserts past her to see what she thought of them.

Grabbing her purse, she began to dig through the chaotic interior to locate her phone.

"Why is it always on the bottom?" she asked the dog, who just looked at her as if she was speaking in some foreign language. "You're no help," she murmured. "Ah, here it is." Triumphantly, she pulled the phone out of the depths of her purse.

Just before she pressed "accept" she automatically looked at the caller ID.

The caller's name jumped out at her: Christopher Whitman.

Chapter Eight

Lily pressed the green band labeled "accept" on her cell. "Hello?"

"Lily, hi, it's Chris." The deep voice on the other end of the line seemed to fill the very air around her the moment he began to speak. "I'm afraid there's been a change of plans. I'm not going to be able to make it over to your place."

"I kind of figured that part out already," she told him, trying very hard to sound casual about the whole thing, rather than disappointed, which she was. While she had more or less assumed that he wasn't going to come over, she had to admit that there was still a small part of her that had held out hope when she saw that the incoming call was from him.

Ordinarily, Christopher would have just left it at that, ending the call by saying goodbye with no further explanation.

But he didn't want to, not this time.

He'd always been nothing if not honest with himself and he had to admit that this was *not* an ordinary, run-of-the-mill situation. Not for him. He wasn't sure just what it actually was at this point, but he did know that he wanted to be able to keep all his options open—just in case.

"Rhonda was hit by a car," he told Lily.

"Oh, my God, how awful." Lily's sympathies instantly rushed to the foreground, completely wiping out every other emotion in its path, even though the person's name meant nothing to her. He hadn't mentioned the woman before, but she obviously meant a great deal to him. "Is there anything at all that I can do to help?"

"No, I've got it covered," he told her. "But I'd like to take a rain check on that home training session if it's okay with you."

"Sure, absolutely." Her words came out in a rush. The thought of car accidents always ran a cold chill down her spine. She could relate to loss easily. At times she felt *too* easily. "Don't give it another thought. Go be with Rhonda."

Whoever that was, she added silently.

It occurred to her that she had no idea if Christopher was talking about a friend, a relative, or possibly a girlfriend, or someone more significant to him than that. What she did know was that the event itself sounded absolutely terrible and she really felt for him.

It did cause her to wonder how he could have even spared a single thought about helping her to start housebreaking Jonathan at a time like this. The man either had an exceedingly big heart, or she was missing something here.

"I really hope she pulls through, Christopher," Lily told him in all sincerity.

She heard silence on the other end. Just when she'd decided that the connection had been lost or terminated, she heard Christopher respond.

"Yeah, me, too."

"Let me know how she's doing—if you get a chance," Lily added hastily. The last thing she wanted was for him to think she was being clingy or pushy at a time like this.

It might have been her imagination, but she thought he sounded a little strange, or possibly slightly confused, as he said, "Yeah, sure." And then his voice became more urgent and almost gruff as she heard him tell her, "I have to go."

The line went dead.

She stood looking at her cell phone for a long moment, even though there was no one on the other end anymore.

"Guess it really is just the two of us, Jonathan." The Labrador made a yipping sound, as if in agreement.

Putting her cell phone down on the coffee table, Lily went to the kitchen to see if her landline's answering machine had any incoming calls on it. She hadn't had a chance to check today's messages and wondered if there were any messages on it from a frantic dog owner who had seen one of her posters.

She had a total of three calls waiting to be heard. For a moment, she stood looking at the blinking light, considering erasing the calls without playing them.

Lily reasoned that if she didn't hear the message, she wouldn't be responsible for not returning the call.

C'mon, Lil, since when is ignorance the kind of excuse you want to hide behind? You were eager enough to get rid of Mr. Ball of Fur when you first found him, remember? You wouldn't have posted all those flyers everywhere if you weren't.

While that was true enough then, she'd had a change of heart in these past few hours. Actually, now that she thought of it, her change of heart had been ongoing and gradual.

With all the problems that having this puppy in her life generated, she still found herself reluctant to just hand him over to some stranger, to in effect close her eyes and banish him from her life.

Lily shook her head, looking at the puppy again. It was amazing to her how quickly she could get used to another creature roaming around in her space.

"You're getting attached again, Lil," she reprimanded herself sternly. "You know that was something you didn't want happening."

Well, whether or not she wanted it, Lily thought, looking down at the dog again, it was now official. She *liked* this moving repository of continually falling fur. *Really* liked him.

"So, what do you want to do first?" she asked Jonathan.

And then her eyes widened as she saw his tail go up in that peculiar way he had of making it look like one half of a squared parenthesis. The next moment, she remembered the only time he did that was when he wanted to eliminate wastes from his body.

"Oh, no, no, no, you don't," she insisted.

Grabbing him by his collar—his leash was temporarily missing in action—keeping her fingers as loose as she could within the confining space, she quickly pulled the dog to the rear of the house and ultimately, to the sliding glass back door.

All the while she kept repeating only one order: "Hold it, hold it, hold it!"

She finally stopped saying that the moment she got Jonathan into the backyard. And that was when the energetic puppy let loose. She would have preferred he hadn't made his deposit on the cement patio instead of in the grass just beyond that strip, but in her opinion that was still a whole lot better than having that same thing transpire on the rug or—heaven forbid—the travertine in the kitchen. The latter would become permanently stained if she wasn't extremely quick about cleaning up every last trace of Jonathan's evacuation process.

"You finished?" she asked the dog. As if in response, he trotted back to the sliding glass door, wanting readmittance to the house. "Okay, I'll take that as a yes," she told the animal gamely. "But I want to hear the moment you think you have another overwhelming urge to part company with your breakfast or any of those treats you all but mugged me for in the park."

Acting as if his mistress had lapsed into silence rather than putting him on notice, Jonathan immediately began sniffing around the corners of the room, making no secret of the fact that he was foraging.

He was able to stick his nose in and under all the tight spots, where the cabinets just fell short of meeting the floor. Crumbs had a habit of residing there and

Jonathan was hunting crumbs in lieu of snaring any bigger game.

Lily observed his progress. "You're not going to find anything," she warned the animal. "I keep a very clean house—which means that if you have any further ideas about parting ways with your fur—*don't.* I've got better things to do than vacuum twice a day because you shed 24/7." She turned toward the pantry. "C'mon, I'll give you your dinner—and then I'd appreciate it if you just stretched out over there on the floor by the sofa and went to sleep."

She put Jonathan's food out first, then went to fix something for herself.

The puppy, she noticed out of the corner of her eye, instantly vacuumed up what she'd put into his bowl. Finished, he came over to sit at her feet in the kitchen, waiting for her to either drop something on the floor or pity him enough to share her dinner with him.

"Eye me all you want with those big, sad, puppy eyes of yours," she told him firmly. "It's not happening. While I'm in charge of taking care of you, you're not about to turn into some huge treat-based blimp."

If he understood her—or appreciated her looking out for his health—Jonathan gave her no indication of it. Instead, he seemed to turn into just a massive, needy, walking stomach, ready to desperately sell his little doggie soul for a morsel of food.

Lily had every intention of remaining firm. She held out for as long as she could, looking everywhere but down as she ate. But he got to her. She could *feel* Jonathan pathetically staring at her. And while she knew she was partially responsible inasmuch as she was reading into that expression, she found she couldn't hold out against the canine indefinitely.

With a sigh, she broke off a piece of the sandwich she settled on having and put it on the floor in front of Jonathan. It was gone, disappearing behind his lips faster than she could have executed a double take. She'd barely sat up straight in the chair again.

Looking at the animal, Lily could only shake her head incredulously. "Certainly wouldn't want to be marooned on a deserted island with the likes of you. Two days into it and you'd be eyeing me like I was a pile of raw pork chops—center cut," she added for good measure.

Jonathan barked and she was sure that he was voicing his agreement.

After clearing away the two dishes and the bowl that she had used, Lily found herself way too wound up as well as just too restless to go to bed or even to watch some mundane television program with the hopes that *it* would put her to sleep.

It was Sunday night and as a rule, there was simply nothing worthwhile watching on any of the countless cable channels that she received at that time.

Still, it was far too quiet without the TV, so she switched it on as she washed off the dishes. She kept it on as soothing background noise, glancing at it occasionally just to see if anything interesting turned up.

It never did.

Without anything to watch and with her new four-footed companion sleeping in the corner, Lily did what she always did when she needed to unwind.

She baked.

She started by taking out everything that might lend

itself to baking pastries and lining up the various containers, boxes and jars, large and small, on the far side of the kitchen counter. Seeing what she had to work with, Lily decided what to make.

She was on her third batch of Bavarian-style pastries—low-fat just to prove her point that baking didn't necessarily mean fattening—when she heard the doorbell ring.

The dog's head, she noticed, instantly went up. The dog had gone from zero to sixty in half a second. Jonathan was wide-awake and completely alert.

"Hold that pose, I might need you," she told Jonathan.

Wiping her hands, she went to the front door. Her furry shadow came with her. She didn't bother wasting time by telling him to stay. Having him there beside her generated an aura of safety that had been missing from her life for a while now. Mentally, she crossed her fingers and hoped it wasn't anyone in response to the flyer.

Instead of looking through the peephole, which she found usually distorted the person on the other side of the door, she called out, "Who is it and what are you doing here?"

"Dr. Chris Whitman and I've come to apologize."

Lily's heart ramped up its pace. She fumbled with the lock as she flipped it.

"You already apologized. Don't you remember?" she asked as she opened the door for him. "When you called to tell me you weren't coming, you apologized over the phone."

He remembered, but it hadn't seemed nearly adequate enough to him. And besides, after what he'd just been through, he didn't want to immediately go home to his empty house. He wanted to see a friendly face, talk to a friendly person—and relax in her company. The very fact that he did was a surprise to him since toward the end, he felt nothing but relief to get out of his relationship with Irene.

But then, Lily wasn't Irene. "Then I've come to apologize again," he amended. "And I'm still Dr. Chris Whitman," he added cheerfully, referring to her initial inquiry through the door.

"You didn't have to apologize the first time," she told him. "I mean, it was nice that you thought you had to, but I understand. You had a crisis to handle. By the way, how is she doing?"

He nodded, as if to preface what he was about to say with a visual confirmation. "She's actually doing better than I expected. It looks like she's going to pull through."

It had been touch and go for a while there. It wasn't as if this was the first operation he'd ever performed but it was by far the most demanding and he had done extensive volunteer work at several animal shelters. The five-year-old Irish setter had required a great deal of delicate work.

"That's wonderful news," Lily said, genuinely pleased. She had to raise her voice because Jonathan had decided to become vocal. The animal obviously felt that he was being ignored by the two people in the room, most especially by the man he had taken such a shine to. "But what are you doing here? Shouldn't you be back at the hospital with her?"

Christopher crouched down to scratch the puppy

behind his ears. Jonathan fell over on the floor, clearly in ecstasy.

"Under normal circumstances," Christopher agreed, "I might have stayed the night, but Lara's there. She volunteered to take over this shift. And my number's on speed dial if anything comes up."

That was rather an odd way to put it, Lily thought. Out loud she repeated, "Lara?" Another woman? Just how many women were part of this man's life?

"Yes." He realized that he probably hadn't properly introduced Lily to everyone by name the one time she'd been at his animal hospital. "She's one of the animal techs. You met her the other day when you brought Jonny in to see me."

Lily came to a skidding halt mentally. She put up her hand to stop the flow of his words for a minute. She needed to get her head—not to mention facts—straight.

"You have one of your animal techs watching over Rhonda?" Lily asked incredulously, trying her best to unscramble what Christopher was telling her.

"Yes. Why? What's wrong?" he asked, mystified by the very strange expression that Lily had on her face right now. "It's not like this is her first time."

Well, the only way she was going to clear this up was by asking some very basic questions, Lily decided. "What relation is Rhonda to you? I know it's none of my business, but I'm getting a very strong feeling that we're not on the same page here—"

He'd drink to that, Christopher thought.

"Hold it," he ordered out loud. "Back up." He really wasn't sure he'd heard her correctly. Or had he? "What did you just ask me?"

He was angry because she was prying, Lily thought.

She didn't want to jeopardize her relationship with Christopher. She needed him to help her with the puppy. She just wasn't good at these sorts of things, despite her best intentions.

"Sorry, I stepped over the line, I guess," she told him. "I was just trying to get things straight, but if you don't want to tell me about Lara, or Rhonda, that's your right and I—"

This misunderstanding was getting way out of hand, Christopher realized. The only way to stop this rolling snowflake from becoming a giant, insurmountable snowball to end all snowballs was just to blurt out the truth to Lily, which he did—as fast as possible.

"Rhonda's my neighbor's Irish setter," he explained in as few words as he could. "Josh called me in a panic just as I was driving to your place, said someone driving erratically had hit Rhonda and then just kept on going. She was alive, but had lost a lot of blood. I couldn't turn him down."

Rhonda was a dog? The thought presented itself to her in huge capital letters. The rush of relief that ushered those words in was almost overwhelming. She did her best to refrain from analyzing it. She wasn't equipped for that right now.

"Of course you couldn't." She said the words so fiercely, at first he thought that Lily was putting him on.

But one look into her eyes and he knew she was being completely serious.

And completely lovable while she was at it, he couldn't help thinking.

Christopher only realized much later that his real undoing began at that very minute.

Just as hers did for her.

For Lily, it was realizing that the man who was help-ing her discover the right way to train Jonathan wasn't just someone who was kind when it was convenient for him to be that way, or because he was trying to score points with a woman he'd just met and appeared to be moderately attracted to. The turning point for her, the moment she discovered that she had absolutely no say when it came to being able to properly shield her heart from being breeched, was in finding out that Christo-pher was selfless across the board, especially when it came to animals who needed him.

Her heart went up for sale and was simultaneously taken off the market by that same man in that very small instant of time.

Instantly distracted, Christopher stopped talking and took a deep breath. His question was fairly rhetori-cal because he had a hunch that he knew the answer to it. "What is that fantastic smell?"

It was very hard to keep her face from splitting in half; her smile was that wide and it just continued to widen. It had swiftly reached her eyes when she sug-gested, "Why don't you come into the kitchen and see for yourself?"

Turning on her heel, she led the way into her small kitchen. She didn't realize at the time that there was a bounce to her step.

But Christopher did.

In keeping with the kitchen's compact size, there was an island in the middle, but a small one, just large enough to accommodate two of the three trays she'd placed in the oven earlier. She had taken the two trays out while the third one was still baking.

The closer he came, the stronger the aroma seemed to be. His appetite was firmly aroused and Christopher immediately transformed into a kid walking into his favorite candy shop. "Are those the same pastries you made the other day?"

"Some are, some aren't. I like to mix it up," she confessed.

The pastries on the trays were still warm and were most definitely emitting a siren song as he stared at them.

"Are these all for work?" he asked, circling the trays on the island slowly.

"No, they're for me," she corrected. "Not to eat," she explained quickly. "Baking relaxes me. I usually give them away after I finish." Gesturing toward the trays, she asked, "Would you like to sample one?"

She got as far as gesturing before he took her up on the offer he'd assumed she'd been about to make.

Chapter Nine

"You are, without a doubt, an amazingly gifted young woman."

Christopher uttered the unabashed praise the minute he had finished savoring his very first bite of the pastry he had randomly chosen off the nearest tray. The pastry was filled with cream whipped into fluffy peaks and laced with just enough Amaretto to leave a very pleasant impression. It was practically light enough to levitate off the tray.

"I bake," she said, shrugging carelessly. Lily was warmed by his praise, but she didn't want to make it seem as if she was letting his compliment go to her head.

"No," Christopher corrected her. "My late mother, God bless her, 'baked.' Her desserts, when she made them, always tasted of love, but they were predictable, and while good, they weren't 'special.' Yours are definitely special. You don't just 'bake,' you *create*. There's a big difference."

Christopher paused as he indulged himself a little more, managing to eat almost three quarters of the small pastry before he went on.

"You know, I'm usually one of those people who eat to live, not live to eat. Nobody could *ever* accuse me of being a foodie or whatever those people who love to regale other people with their so-called 'food adventures' like to call themselves. But if I had access to something like this whenever I felt like indulging in a religious experience, I'd definitely change my affiliation—not to mention that I'd probably become grossly overweight. Speaking of which," Christopher went on, switching subjects as he eyed her, "why aren't you fat?" he asked.

"I already told you, I don't eat what I make." Then, before he could say that he had a hard time believing that, she admitted, "Oh, I sample a little here, a dab there, to make sure I'm not going to make someone throw up, but I've just never felt the inclination to polish off a tray of pastries."

Christopher's expression told her that he was having a hard time reconciling that with his own reaction to the end product of her culinary efforts.

"If I were you," he told her, "I'd have a serious talk with myself, because your stubborn half is keeping you from having nothing short of a love affair with your taste buds." He licked the last of the whipped cream from his fingertips, discovering he craved more. "How *did* you come up with these?" he asked, waving his hand at the less-than-full tray of pastries that was closest to him on the counter.

Her method was no big secret, either. It was based on a practical approach.

"It's a very simple process, really. I just gather together a bunch of ingredients and see where they'll take me," she told him.

As if to back up her explanation, Lily indicated the containers, bottles and boxes that had been pressed into service and were now all huddled together on the far side of the counter.

He thought that was rather a strange way to phrase it. But creative people had a very different thought process.

"That means what?" he asked her, curious about her process. "You stare at them until they suddenly speak to you?"

"Not in so many words, but yes, maybe. Why?"

He shook his head, still marveling at her stripped-down approach to creating something so heavenly. With very little effort, he could have easily consumed half a dozen pastries until he exploded.

"Just trying to familiarize myself with your creative process," he answered, then added, "I've never been in the presence of a magician before."

"And you aren't now. It's not magic, it's baking. And that, by the way," she said, indicating the pastry he'd just had, "was one of my low-fat pastries."

He stared at her, undecided if she was telling him the truth or putting him on. "You're kidding."

"Not when it comes to calories," she answered with solemnity.

"Low-fat?" he asked again, looking at the rest of the pastries.

"Low-fat," she confirmed. "Told you you couldn't tell the difference."

Christopher shook his head, clearly impressed. "Now that's really *inspired* baking," he told her with just a hint of wonder.

If he wanted to flatter her, who was she to fight it? Lily thought.

"Okay, I'll go with that." She carefully moved around Jonathan, who appeared to be hanging on his hero's every word. "Now, can I fix you some dinner to go with your 'magical' dessert?" she asked.

He shook his head. "I'm good," he told her. When she raised an eyebrow, waiting for him to explain, he said, "I grabbed a burger on the way over here. I didn't want to put you out."

"Did you eat the burger you grabbed?" she asked. "Because I can still make you something a little more edible than a fast-food hamburger."

He liked the way she crinkled her nose in what appeared to be unconscious disdain of the entire fast-food industry. "I'm sure you can, but the burger filled the hole in my stomach for the time being. Besides, that rain check I mentioned earlier was supposed to be for dinner, too. Dinner out," he emphasized.

"You don't have to wait to be seated if we have dinner in," she pointed out gently. Lily viewed all cooking as an outlet for her and she thoroughly enjoyed doing it. She wanted to convince him that this definitely wasn't "putting her out."

"Don't you like being waited on?" he asked Lily.

"Not particularly," she admitted. Then, not wanting

to sound like some sort of a weirdo, she told him, "Although I'm not overly fond of washing dishes."

"Do you?" he asked in surprise. "Wash dishes," he elaborated when he didn't get a response.

"Yes." Why was he asking? She thought she'd just said as much.

He glanced over toward the appliance next to her stove. "Is your dishwasher broken?"

She automatically glanced at it because he had, even though she didn't need to in order to answer his question. "I don't know, I've never used it. There's just me and it doesn't seem right to run all that water just for a few plates."

There was a solution to that. "Then wait until you have enough dishes to fill up the dishwasher," he suggested.

"That seems even less right." Lily suppressed a shiver as she envisioned stacking dirty plates on top of one another.

"Leaving a bunch of dirty dishes lying around until there's enough for a full load sounds awful. Either way is offensive," she said with feeling. "It's a lot easier if I just wash as I go. My mom taught me that," she told him out of the blue. "This was her house—*our* house, as she liked to put it even though I never paid a dime toward its purchase. My mom handled everything," she recalled fondly. "Held down two, sometimes three jobs, just to pay the bills.

"If there was anything extra, she proudly put it toward my college fund. By the time I was set to go to college, there was a lot of money in that little slush fund of hers. Enough to set me on the road to any college I wanted."

Caught up in her reminiscing, Christopher asked, "So where did you go?"

He watched as her smile faded. Sorrow all but radiated from her. "I didn't. That was the year my mother got sick. Really sick. At first, the doctors she went to see all told her it was in her head, that she was just imagining it. And then one doctor decided to run a series of more complex tests on her—which was when Mom found out that she wasn't imagining it. She had brain cancer." She said the diagnosis so quietly, Christopher wouldn't have heard her if he wasn't standing so close to her.

"By the time they found it, it had metastasized to such a degree that it was too hard to cut out and get it all. They went in, did what they could, and then Mom said, 'No more.' She told them that she wanted to die at home, in one piece. And she did," Lily concluded proudly, her voice wavering slightly as she fought back the tears that always insisted on coming whenever she talked about her mother at any length.

"I used the money she had set aside for my college fund to pay off her medical bills." Lily shrugged helplessly, as if paying off the bills had somehow ultimately helped her cope with her loss. "It seemed only right to me."

Lily stopped talking for a second to wipe away the tears that insisted on seeping out from the corners of her eyes.

"Sorry, I get pretty emotional if I talk about my mother for more than two minutes." She attempted to smile and was only partially successful. "I didn't mean to get all dark and somber on you."

"That's okay," he assured her. "I know what it feels

like to lose a mother who's sacrificed everything for you." She looked up at him. "You'd trade every last dime you had just to spend one more day with her. But you can't, so you do the next best thing. You prove to the world that she was right about you. That you *can* do something that counts, to make some sort of a difference. And I have no doubt that somewhere, tucked just out of sight, my mom and yours are watching over us and are pretty satisfied with the people they single-handedly raised," he told her with a comforting smile.

She took in a deep breath, doing her best to get her emotions under control. His words were tremendously comforting to her.

"You think?" she asked.

"I know," he countered. Looking at her, he saw the telltale trail forged by a stray teardrop. "You missed one."

With that, he lifted her chin with the tip of his finger, tilting it slightly. Using just his thumb, Christopher very gently wiped the stray tear away from the corner of her eye.

Their eyes met for one very long moment and her breath felt as if it had become solid in her throat as she held it.

Waiting.

Hoping.

Trying not to.

And then everything else, her surroundings, the kitchen, the pastries, even the overenergized puppy that was responsible for bringing them together in the first place, it just faded into the background like so much inconsequential scenery.

She was acutely aware of her heart and the ramped-up rhythm it had attained.

Christopher lowered his mouth to hers and ever so lightly, like a sunbeam barely touching her skin, he kissed her.

The next moment, he drew back and she thought for a second that the sound of her heart, beating wildly, had driven him back.

"Sorry, I didn't mean to take advantage of you like that," he told her, still cupping her cheek with the palm of his hand.

Her voice felt as if it was going to crack at any second as she told him, "You didn't. And there's nothing to be sorry about, except…"

"Except?" he prodded.

Lily shook her head, not wanting to continue. She was only going to embarrass herself—and him—if she said anything further. "I've said too much."

"No," he contradicted, "you've said too little. 'Except' what?" he coaxed.

Lily wavered. Maybe he did deserve to know. So she told him.

"Except maybe it didn't last long enough," she said, her voice hardly above a whisper, her cheeks burning and threatening to turn a deep pink.

"Maybe it didn't," he agreed. "Let's see if I get it right this time," he murmured just before his mouth came down on hers for a second time.

This time nothing happened in slow motion. This time, she could feel the heat travel through her as if its path had been preset with a thin line of accelerant, a line that ran between the two of them as well as over the length of her.

They'd been sitting at the counter on stools that swiveled and were now turned toward one another. Lily caught herself sliding from the stool, her arms entwined around the back of Christopher's neck.

He stood up at the same moment that she had gotten off the stool.

The length of her body slid against his. His ridges and contours registered with acute details. All the electricity between them crackled with a fierceness that was all but staggering.

He savored the sweetness of her mouth in a far more profound way than he had savored the flour-and-cream creations she'd made. The Amaretto in the pastry had been just the tiniest bit heady. The taste of her lips was far more intoxicating.

So much so that it sent out alarms all throughout his body, warning him that he was walking into something he might not be prepared for. Something he might not be equipped to handle at this juncture of his life, all things considered.

The magnitude of his feelings right at this moment was enough to make Christopher back away, concerned about the consequences that waited for him if he wasn't careful.

It wasn't easy, but he forced himself to draw back again.

"Maybe I better go," he told her, the words that emerged sounding low and almost gravelly.

She needed time to pull herself together. Time to try to understand just what it was that was going on here—aside from her complete undoing. Time to fix the shield around her heart because it had seriously cracked.

"Maybe you'd better," she agreed.

He tried to remember what had brought him here in the first place. It was difficult to get a fix on his thoughts; they were scattered and unfocused. All he was aware of was how much he wanted her.

"I just wanted to tell you in person why I backed out this afternoon," he finally managed to say.

"I appreciate that," she told him, then added belatedly, "I appreciate everything you've done."

Her wits managed to finally come together. The relief she experienced at being able to think again was incredible. She almost felt as if she was in full possession of her mental faculties again. Or at least enough to be able to carry on a normal conversation. Even so, she didn't want to push herself and have it all fall apart on her again.

Something about this man threatened her carefully constructed world and if she wasn't on her guard, all the work she had put in to keeping her heart out of danger's reach would go up in smoke.

"Why don't you take one or two for the road? Or more if you like," Lily suggested, doing her very best to sound casual. It wasn't easy talking with one's heart in one's throat.

"One or two for the road?" he echoed. They'd just been locked in a kiss, so was she talking about those? he wondered, looking at her uncertainly.

"Or more," she repeated again. "I can wrap up as many pastries as you'd like to take home with you. Maybe even give a couple to your poor neighbor for what he's just gone through."

And then it all clicked into place. She was talking about the pastries, not about kissing him again. Christopher laughed—more at himself and at what he had thought she was saying than at what Lily was actually telling him.

"You're being too generous," he said.

She didn't quite see it that way. "I like to spread smiles around and these pastries make people smile."

"That they do," he wholeheartedly agreed. He looked over toward the remaining two and a half trays. "I can completely attest to that."

"Then let me give you some." It was no longer a suggestion but a statement of intent.

She had a total of eight pastries wrapped, placed in a cardboard container and ready to go within a couple of minutes.

"You sure you don't want more?" she asked. He'd stopped her when she had reached for the ninth pastry, saying eight was already too much.

"I want them all," he told her honestly. *And more than just pastries right now,* he added silently. He concentrated, determined to keep even a hint of the latter thought from registering on his face. "But in the spirit of sharing, what you just packed up for me to take with me is more than enough." Not wanting to leave it just at that, he told her, "I can come by tomorrow afternoon if you like—and we can pick up where we left off."

Belatedly, Christopher realized he had worded that last line rather poorly, allowing her to misunderstand his meaning. "Left off training Jonny," he tacked on awkwardly.

He had never been a smooth talker—the type who was able to sell ice cubes to polar bears—but he had never had this much trouble saying what he meant.

This woman had definitely scrambled his ability to communicate. Why was that?

He had no hard-and-fast answer—and the one that did suggest itself made him nervous.

"That would be very nice of you," Lily was saying as she walked him to the front door. Jonathan came along, prancing around, all but tripping both of them as he wove in and out between them. "I'll bake you something else next time," she promised with a smile that completely seeped under his skin.

Christopher laughed, shaking his head as he opened the front door. "You do that and I'm going to have to start shopping in the husky-men section of the local department store."

Her eyes swept over him, as if to verify what she already knew. "You have a long way to go before that happens," she assured him.

"Not as long as you think," he replied just before he turned and walked out. He didn't trust himself to stand on the doorstep one second longer.

She made him want things he had no business wanting. Things that, if he recalled correctly—and he did—would only ultimately promise to lead to an unhappy ending sometime in the near future.

Been there, done that, he thought as he got into his car and drove away.

As if to contradict him, the warm scent coming from the pastries seemed to rise up and intensify, filling his car. It made him think of Lily all the way home.

Chapter Ten

There wasn't a single position on her bed that felt comfortable enough for her to fall asleep for more than a few minutes at a time. And when she actually *did* manage to fall asleep, she wound up dreaming about what was keeping her awake, perpetuating her dilemma.

She dreamed about a magnetic pair of blue eyes that pulled her in and thick, dirty-blond hair that curled just enough to make her fingers itchy to run through it.

And at the end of each and every one of these mini-dreams Lily would experience a deep, dark feeling of bereavement, of being suddenly, irreversibly left behind, to continue on alone.

She felt as if her insides had been hollowed out by a sharp, serrated carving knife. Then she'd bolt upright, awake and damp with perspiration despite the fact that the night air was cool tonight.

Alone in her bedroom, her knees drawn up against her chest as if her body was forming an impenetrable circle, Lily recognized her nightmares for what they were, what they signified: fear. Fear of caring, fear of experiencing the consequences that came from allowing herself to care about someone.

Was she crazy to even *think* that she could have some sort of a relationship without paying the ultimate terrible price that relationship demanded? If you danced, then you were required to pay the piper. She knew that and she desperately didn't want to have anything at all to do with the piper.

Not ever again.

The best thing was just to remain strangers, the way they were now.

Finally, at six in the morning, Lily gave up all attempts of trying to get even a solid hour of uninterrupted sleep.

With a deep sigh, she threw off her covers and got out of her extremely rumpled bed. Glancing at the tangled sheets and bunched-up comforter, it occurred to her that her bed looked as if it had been declared a war zone.

Maybe it had been, she thought ruefully. Except that there had been no winner declared.

She normally never left her bedroom in the morning without first making her bed, but this morning, she abandoned the bed entirely. She just wanted to get out of the house.

Maybe some fresh air would do her some good.

Putting on a pair of jeans and donning a light sweater, she announced to the puppy that had insisted on sleeping on her bedroom floor, "We're going out for a walk, Jonathan."

Fully awake in less than an instant, the Labrador half ran, half slid down the stairs and then darted around until she reached the landing to join him. Picking the leash up where she'd dropped it by the staircase, Lily hooked it onto the dog's collar. At the last minute she remembered to take a bag with her just in case she got lucky and the dog actually relieved himself while they were out.

Taking Jonathan for a walk was yet another exercise in patience. It consisted of all but dashing down one residential street after another, followed by periods of intense sniffing that lasted so long Lily finally had to literally drag the puppy away—at which point he would abruptly dash again.

This theme and variation of extremes went on for close to an hour before Lily finally decided that she'd had enough and wanted to head back to the house.

Just before they reached their destination, Jonathan abruptly stopped dead, nearly causing her to collide with him because of the shift in momentum. When she turned toward the dog to upbraid him for almost tripping her, she saw that the puppy was relieving himself.

She realized that meant she didn't need to be so vigilant for the next few hours. "I guess I'm home free for half the day, right?"

The Labrador had no opinion one way or the other. He was far too busy investigating what he had just parted with. Lily pulled him back before he managed to get too close to it.

This having a dog was going to take some getting

used to, she thought, elbowing the puppy out of the way in order to clean up after him.

A *lot* of getting used to, she amended after she finished with her task.

Lily got back to her house just in time to hear her landline ring. Unlocking the door and hurrying inside, she managed to get to the telephone a scarce heartbeat before it went to voice mail.

Dropping Jonathan's leash, she picked up the receiver. "Hello?"

There was about a second or so delay before someone answered her. She reacted the moment that she heard his voice.

"Lily, hi. I was just getting ready to leave a message on your machine," the deep voice on the other end told her.

She could feel goose bumps forming on her skin. There was something incredibly intimate and, okay, *arousing* about Christopher's voice on the phone. But that still didn't change her resolve about keeping the man at arm's length. If anything, it strengthened it.

"Now you can leave a message with me," she said, forcing herself to sound as cheerful as she possibly could.

When she heard him draw in a long breath, she knew it couldn't be good. "I'm afraid I'm going to have to cancel today."

She had a feeling, a split second before he said the words, that he was going to bow out. Which was fine, because that was what she wanted.

But if that was the case, why was there this vast,

hard lump of disappointment doing a nosedive in the pit of her stomach?

"I didn't know you had the power to do that," she said, still doing her best to sound light and upbeat. "To cancel an entire day." The silence on the other end made her feel like squirming. "Sorry, that was me just trying to be funny. I didn't mean to interrupt you while you were talking."

He did the worst thing he could have done, Lily thought. He was understanding. "You weren't interrupting, you were being humorous."

Maybe he was canceling because he had another emergency, and she was making wisecracks. Lily felt terrible.

"And you're being nice." She apologized in the best way she knew how. She absolved him of any obligation. "It's okay, about canceling," she added since she knew her words sounded vague. "I understand."

"How can you understand?" Christopher asked. "I haven't told you why I'm canceling yet."

He had a point. Her nerves were making her jump to conclusions. She searched for something plausible to use as an excuse, but came up empty. She went with vague. "I'm sure it's for a good reason."

"I wish it wasn't," he told her honestly. Something had made him go in very early this morning, to check on his neighbor's dog. Rhonda hadn't been as responsive as he would have liked. Further investigation had brought him to this conclusion. "Rhonda had some internal bleeding suddenly start up. I have to go back in and cauterize the wound, then sew her up again. When I finish, I want to watch her for a few hours, just to be sure she's on the mend this time. That means I won't be coming over today to work with Jonathan."

That he could even think about that when he had an emergency on his hands made her feel that he was a very exceptional person. She didn't want him to feel as if he was letting her down in any way.

"Well, as it turns out, Jonathan and I went out for a long walk this morning and he decided he couldn't hold it long enough to come back to the house to make a mess, so he went outside."

Tickled at the way she'd narrated her latest adventure with the dog, Christopher laughed. "Congratulations. But you do realize you're not out of the woods yet, right? The process has to be repeated—a lot—before it becomes ingrained. Did you remember to praise him after he finished going?"

Lily pressed her lips together. She *knew* she'd forgotten something. "Is praising him important?" she asked, hoping he'd tell her that it was just a minor detail.

"It is—and I'll take that as a no. Next time Jonny goes, praise him to the hilt and tell him what a wonderful puppy he is. Trust me," he assured her, "it works wonders."

She sighed, glancing at the dog who had plopped down at her feet, apparently content to lie there, at least for the moment. "I'll remember next time."

"Listen, I need to go, but you can still drop Jonny off here on your way to work tomorrow—unless you feel confident enough to leave him alone at your house," he added, not wanting her to think he was talking her into leaving the dog at his clinic for the day.

"I'll drop him off," she said quickly, relieved that he hadn't taken back his offer. She wasn't naive enough to think that one success meant that the puppy's behavior was permanently altered. "And thank you."

"Don't mention it. Now I've really got to go," he told her again.

Christopher hung up before she had a chance to say goodbye.

Mixed feelings scrambled through her as Lily hung up the receiver. She didn't know whether to be relieved that Christopher wasn't coming over—relieved that she wouldn't find herself alone with him—or upset for the very same exact reason.

Jonathan barked and she realized that he was no longer lying down at her feet. The bark sounded rather urgent. She had a feeling that he was asking for his breakfast. Christopher—and her present ambivalent dilemma—wouldn't have been part of her life if Jonathan hadn't been on her doorstep that fateful morning.

"Life was a lot simpler before you came into it, Jonathan," she told the puppy.

Jonathan just went on barking at her until she began walking to the kitchen. Following her, his barking took on a different, almost triumphant intensity.

Lily laughed to herself. Exactly who was training whom here?

She had a sneaking suspicion she knew. Right now, the score was Jonathan one, Lily zero. She took out a can of dog food and popped the top.

The following morning, Lily nearly drove right past the turn she was supposed to make to get to the animal hospital. At the last minute, she slowed down and deliberately made the right-hand turn.

Less than a mile later, she was driving into the

rather busy upscale strip mall where Christopher's animal hospital was located.

Lily had come close to driving past the initial right-hand turn not because she had a poor sense of direction, but because she had a strong sense of survival. The more she interacted with the handsome, sexy veterinarian, the more she was going to *want* to interact with him—and that sort of thing would lead to an attachment she told herself that she ultimately didn't want.

But, as always, stronger still was her utter disdain for behaving like a coward. It didn't matter whether no one knew or not. *She* would know and that was all that really counted. Once she began going off in that direction, there would be no end to the things she would find excuses to run from.

She didn't want to live like that, didn't want fear to get the upper hand over her or to govern any aspect of her life.

If she allowed it to happen once, then it would be sure to happen again. And next time, it would be easier to just back away from something. Before she'd know it, her individuality would be forfeited, buried beneath an ever-growing mountain of things for her to fear and to avoid *because* of that fear.

At that point, she wouldn't be living, merely existing. Life, her mother had always told her, had to be relished and held on to with both hands. It wasn't easy, but it was definitely worth it.

Conquering this fear of involvement because she feared being left alone had to be on the top of her to-do list. Otherwise, she was doomed to be lonely right from the beginning.

* * *

The receptionist, Erika, looked up, a prepasted smile on her lips as she said, "Hello." And then recognition set in. Once it did, the woman's smile became genuine.

"Hi, Dr. Whitman said you might stop by." Coming out from behind the desk, Erika turned her attention to Jonathan. "Hi, boy. Have you come to spend the day with us?"

"I guess I'm boarding him," Lily said, handing over the leash to the receptionist.

"Not technically," Erika told her. "If you were boarding him, there'd be a charge. Dr. Whitman said there'd be no charge, so Jonathan's just visiting," she concluded with a warm smile.

While she was grateful, that didn't sound quite right to Lily. "Do you often have pets come by who are just visiting?"

"Jonathan's our first," the receptionist answered honestly. Then, sensing that the Labrador's owner might be having second thoughts about leaving him for the day, Erika told her, "Don't worry, Jonathan will be just fine here. We could stand to have a mascot hanging around the place. Right, Jonathan?"

The dog responded by wagging his tail so hard it thumped on the floor.

"I'm not worried."

Truthfully, Lily wasn't having second thoughts about leaving Jonathan. The second thoughts involved her running into Christopher. She wondered if he was already here, and if he was, why hadn't he come out?

Maybe it was better if he didn't, she decided in the next moment.

Right, like that's going to change anything about your reaction to the man.

She pressed her lips together and blocked out the little voice in her head that insisted on being logical. It was time for her to say goodbye to the puppy and get going.

Yet for some reason, her feet weren't getting the message. They remained planted exactly where they were, as if they were glued to the spot.

She allowed herself just one question—and then she was going to leave, she insisted. Really.

"How's Rhonda?"

Holding on to Jonathan's leash, Erika looked at her in surprise. "You know Rhonda?"

Serves you right for saying anything.

"Not exactly," Lily admitted. "But Chris—Dr. Whitman," she amended quickly, "mentioned that she was his neighbor's dog and that she'd been hit by a car the other day. I was just wondering if she was doing any better now."

Erika actually beamed.

"Oh, she's doing *much* better. Would you like to see her?"

The response, followed by the question, didn't come from Erika. It came from the veterinarian who had come out of the back of the clinic and was now standing directly behind her.

Lily turned around to face him, trying to act as if her heart hadn't just given up an extra beat—or maybe three.

"Oh, I don't want to put you out any more than I already have—" She saw the puzzled expression on

Christopher's face, so she explained, "By leaving Jonathan here."

"You're not putting anyone out leaving Jonny here," he assured her. He ruffled the dog's head before pushing open the swinging door that led to the back of the clinic. "Rhonda's back here," Christopher told her.

He stood, holding the rear door open with his back, waiting for her to cross the threshold and come follow him.

Lily had no choice but to do as he asked. To do otherwise would have been rude.

Christopher led the way to where the Irish setter was recuperating from her second surgery. The dog was dozing and looked almost peaceful—except for the bandages wrapped around part of her hindquarters. The dog was in a large cage.

"Isn't she cramped, staying in there?" Lily asked, looking at him. Her voice was filled with sympathy.

"Right now, I don't want her moving around too much," he explained. "If I think she's responding properly to the surgery and her stitches are healing well, I'll have her transferred to the run before I have my neighbor take her home with him."

"The run?" Lily echoed.

Rather than explain verbally, Christopher quietly took her by the hand and drew her over to another area of the hospital.

There were three wide enclosures all next to one another. All three were sufficiently wide for a large animal to not just stretch out, but to literally run around if it so chose.

Christopher stood by silently, letting her absorb it

all, then waved his hand at the enclosures. "Hence the term," he explained.

It began making a little more sense, she thought, taking everything in. And then she looked at Christopher again.

"You sure you don't mind my leaving Jonathan here all day?" she asked again.

"I'm sure," he answered. And then he smiled. "Besides, it'll give you a reason to come back."

Why was it that the man could instantly make her heart flutter with just a glance. After all, she wasn't some freshly minted teenager with stars in her eyes. She was an adult who'd endured death and lived life on her own. Heart palpitations over a good-looking man were definitely *not* in keeping with the way she envisioned herself.

There was no one to give her any answers.

Just then, the receptionist popped her head in. Lily noticed that Jonathan was no longer with the woman. "Doctor, Penelope is here for her shots. I put her in Room 3."

"Tell Mrs. Olsen I'll be right in, Erika," he told his receptionist. And then he turned to Lily. "Penelope is a Chihuahua. Giving her injections is a challenge. The needle is almost bigger than she is. Poor thing shakes uncontrollably the minute I walk into the room and she sees me. I hate having any animal afraid of me," he confided as they left the area.

He paused by the swinging door that led to the reception desk. "We're open until six," he told her. "If you need to leave Jonny here longer than that, I'll just take him home with me," he offered.

"Thank you, but that really won't be necessary. I've

got a very understanding boss and she'll let me take off to pick up Jonathan," she told him. "I'll see you before six," she promised.

And with that, Lily hurried out of the animal hospital, moving just a little faster than she might have under normal circumstances.

But even as she reached her vehicle and slid in behind the steering wheel, she had to come to terms with the very basic fact that no matter how quickly she moved, there was no way she was going to come close to outrunning her own thoughts.

Chapter Eleven

Lily felt as if she had never been busier.

Theresa's catering company had not one but two catering events going on, with both taking place that evening.

One event was a fund-raiser for a local charity. It entailed a full seven-course meal and the guest list was for a hundred and fifty-eight people. The other was a celebration on a smaller scale. It was a bridal shower and the only things that were required were champagne and a cake that could feed a group of thirty guests, give or take a few.

Lily worked almost nonstop from the moment she entered the shop until the last dessert was carefully boxed up and sent off on its way.

Without being fully aware of it, she breathed a long sigh of relief. It felt as if she'd been on her feet for at least eighteen hours straight and, although she loved to bake, it was really good to be finished,

"You outdid yourself today," Theresa told her as she oversaw the last of the food being placed in the catering van. Turning from the vehicle, she took a closer look at her pastry chef. "You look really tired, Lily."

Concern elbowed its way to the surface. No matter what else she did or accomplished with her life, Theresa was first and foremost a mother with a mother's sense of priorities. "Do you need someone to drive you home, dear? I don't want you falling asleep behind the wheel. I'd drive you myself but I already have to figure out how to be in two places at once. Three is completely beyond my limit—for now," the older woman added with a twinkle in her eye.

"I'm fine, Theresa," Lily assured the older woman. She didn't want Theresa worrying about her. "Besides, I'm not going straight home."

Halfway out the front door, ready to drive over to the fund-raiser first to make sure that all would go well there, Theresa turned back to her. It was obvious that her interest was piqued.

"Oh?" Her bright eyes pinned Lily in place. "Do you have a date?"

"With the dog," Lily quickly informed her boss with a laugh. "I left Jonathan at the animal hospital before coming here this morning."

"Oh, is he sick?" Since this was partially her idea, to unite Lily with the puppy, she couldn't help feeling responsible for this turn of events.

Lily immediately set her straight. "Oh, no, nothing like that. Christopher, um, Dr. Whitman," she quickly amended, "said I could drop Jonathan off at his office so that he'd be properly looked after while I was gone. Otherwise, he might cause havoc in the house and I really didn't have the heart to stick him into one of those crates."

Theresa cocked her head, still regarding her intently. "You *are* talking about the dog and not the veterinarian, right?" the catering company owner wanted to verify.

Lily couldn't help laughing. Thanks to that, she felt close to rejuvenated as she answered, "Yes, but just for the record, I wouldn't want to put Dr. Whitman into a crate, either."

Theresa inclined her head, agreeing. "I'm sure that he'll be happy to hear that. And now," she announced as the catering van's driver honked to remind her that she had to get going, "I'm overdue getting out of here and have to fly. Enjoy yourself."

Lily felt the instruction was completely misplaced. "I'm only picking up my dog."

A rather ambiguous, mysterious smile graced Theresa's lips. "No reason you can't enjoy that," the older woman tossed over her shoulder just before she finally hurried out the door.

That was definitely a very odd thing to say, Lily thought, staring at the closed door.

But she didn't have any time to puzzle it out. She had a dog to pick up and—Lily glanced at her watch—only half an hour to do it in. The animal hospital closed at six o'clock.

She could make it there in twenty, Lily thought confidently.

She didn't.
Under ordinary circumstances, she could have eas-

ily made it to the animal hospital in the allotted amount of time left. However, ordinary circumstances did *not* involve a three-car collision that caused several blocks to be shut down to through traffic as two ambulances and three tow trucks were dispatched and made their way through the completely clogged area.

Utterly stressed out, the last of her patience all but stripped from her, Lily finally arrived at the Bedford Animal Hospital sixteen minutes after its doors had closed for the evening.

Even so, ever hopeful, Lily parked in the first space she could find, jumped out of her vehicle and ran to the animal hospital's front door. Lily tried turning the knob, but it was securely locked and the lights inside the office were turned off.

Everything was dark.

Now what? Christopher was going to think that she deliberately left the dog with him and wasn't coming back for Jonathan.

That was when she finally saw it.

There was a business envelope with the hospital's return address in the corner taped to the side of the doorjamb. Her name was written across the front in bold block letters.

She lost no time in pulling off the tape and opening the envelope. Inside was a single sheet of paper.

It read: "Lily, had to close up. Couldn't reach you by phone so I'm taking Jonny home with me. If you want to pick him up tonight, here's the address."

Just like the rest of the note, the address on the bottom was printed in block letters, but even bigger than the previous part so that there was no chance that she would have trouble reading it.

Staring at it, she realized that the address was close to her own house. If she wasn't mistaken, the veterinarian's house was just two developments away.

It really was a small world.

With her GPS turned on and engaged to make sure she didn't accidentally go off in the wrong direction, Lily lost no time in driving over to the address in Christopher's note.

She didn't know why, maybe because of his practice, but she had just naturally assumed that Christopher would be living in one of the newer homes that had recently gone up in the area. Once a homey small town built around a state university, Bedford had grown and was still continuing to grow. A thriving city now, it still managed to maintain its small-town feel.

Her GPS brought her to one of the older, more mature neighborhoods. Looking at the address that matched the one in the note, she judged that the house had to be around the same age as the one she lived in. That made the building approximately thirty years old.

After her mother had died, Lily found that she couldn't bear to sell the house. The thought of having another family move in and change everything around had just been too hard for her to cope with at the time. There were just too many memories there for her to part with so easily.

As she slowed down and approached the house, she saw Christopher's car in the driveway. Parking at the curb, Lily got out and made her way to the massive double front doors. The moment she rang the doorbell, she heard barking.

Jonathan.

But the very next moment Lily thought she made

out two distinct barks—or was that three? There was definitely another dog there besides Jonathan. Had her dog learned to play with other dogs? The thought raised other questions in her mind, all having to do with the energetic puppy's safety.

Worried, Lily was about to ring the doorbell a second time when the door suddenly swung open. Christopher was standing inside, one hand on the door, the other holding off not one dog, but three.

The second he realized it was her, he grinned. "So you made it." The way he said it sounded as though congratulations were implied. "I wasn't sure if you'd see the note."

He shouldn't have had to post the note, Lily thought, feeling guilty that he'd had to go to extra trouble on her account. She should have been at the hospital to collect her pet before he'd ever left the place.

Her apology came out in a rush. "I'm sorry. We had two big events going on at the same time then there was a three-car collision and—"

Somewhat overwhelmed by the words and her speed in offering them, Christopher held his hand up as if to physically stop the flow of explanation.

"That's okay, no harm. I would have kept him here overnight if you couldn't come to pick him up for some reason. I did try reaching you before we closed up," he told her. All three attempts went directly to voice mail. Usually there was only one reason for that. "Is your phone off?"

She would have been the first to admit that this had not been her best day. "My cell phone battery died," she said, chagrinncd but owning up to her oversight. "I left it on overnight and forgot to charge it."

Christopher looked amused rather than fazed. "I do the same thing," he told her.

Lily doubted it. She had a feeling the man was only saying that to make her feel better, and he had a tiny bit.

"Jonathan's been making friends with Leopold and Max," he told her, gesturing toward the two Great Danes that were on either side of her puppy like two huge, somewhat messy bookends. "I think they think he's a toy I brought home for them."

"As long as they don't think he's a chew toy or try to bury him in the backyard," Lily quipped, then became serious. "I don't know how to thank you," she began. "Except to just grab his leash and get out of your way."

"No need to hurry off," he countered. His eyes swept over her, backing up his statement. "I'm having pizza delivered. You can stay and have some if you like. There's more than enough to share."

"Pizza?" Lily repeated.

He wasn't quite sure why she looked at him uncertainly. "Yes. You know, that round thing with sauce and cheese. People usually have more things put on top of it."

"I know what pizza is." She looked around at the towering boxes that seemed to be just about everywhere. "Are you having that for dinner because you're busy packing up to move?"

"I'm not packing up," he told her, then asked, "What makes you think I'm moving?"

"There are boxes stacked up all over the place," she said, gesturing toward the nearest cardboard tower. "You're not moving?" she questioned. Then why were all these boxes here?

"I'm not moving *out,*" he corrected. "I'm moving

in. This is—was," he amended, "my mother's house. I thought I'd stay here instead of renting an apartment until I decide if I want to sell the place or not."

She could more than understand how he felt. "So you lost your mother recently." It wasn't a question so much as a conclusion, one voiced with all due sympathy since she vividly recalled how she had felt at the time of her mother's death.

"Feels like it," he admitted. Still, he didn't want the facts getting lost. "But it's been close to five months."

Her eyes swept around the area. The boxes almost made her claustrophobic. In his place, she didn't think she could rest until she got everything put away and the boxes stashed in some recycling bin.

"When did you move in?" she asked him, curious.

"Close to three months," he answered.

He was kidding, she thought. But one look at his chiseled face told her that he was being serious. How could he *stand* it like this?

"Three months? And you haven't unpacked?" she questioned, staring at him.

"Not all of it," he answered vaguely, hoping she didn't want any more details than that.

The truth was, except for some of his clothes, he hadn't unpacked at all. A reluctance had taken hold of him. If he didn't actually unpack his things, he could pretend that somewhere, on some plane, his old life was still intact, maybe also that his mother was still alive. He knew that was far-fetched but the mind didn't always work in a logical, linear fashion.

"I'm doing it slowly. I'm really not much on unpacking," he admitted.

Lily ventured into the next room, which looked a great deal like the room she had initially entered.

"Really? I would have never guessed," she told him, raising her voice so that he could hear her. Coming out again, she made him an offer. "How would you like some help? It goes faster if there're two people unpacking instead of one."

He didn't want to put her out and, if he read that look in her eyes correctly, he definitely didn't want her pity.

"Thanks, but I can handle it."

"No offense, Christopher, but I don't think you can. Besides, it would make me feel that in a way, I'm paying you back for taking care of Jonathan."

The doorbell rang. "Hold that thought," he instructed as he went to answer the door. "Does that mean you'll have some pizza with me?" he asked as he reached for the doorknob.

"Okay, if that's the package deal, then yes, I'll have a slice of pizza—and then get to work," she specified.

Christopher paid the delivery boy, handing him a twenty and telling him to keep the change. Closing the door with his back, he held on to the oversize box with both hands. The pizza inside was still very warm and the aroma that wafted out was mouthwatering.

Lily couldn't take her eyes off the box he was holding.

"That box is huge," she couldn't help commenting.

He glanced down as if seeing it for the first time. It *was* rather large at that. "I thought while I was at it, I might as well get enough to last until tomorrow night, too."

Lily shook her head. "Oh, no, tomorrow night you're having a hot meal," she contradicted.

"This is hot," he told her.

"A *real* hot meal," she emphasized. Since he seemed to be resisting her suggestion, one she was making for the purest of reasons, she further said, "You don't even have to go out of your way to get it. I'll bring it here to you." Once out of her mouth, she found she liked what she'd just come up with. "That way, we can eat as we unpack."

He didn't remember this becoming a two-day joint project. And while he liked the idea of having her come over and sharing another meal with him, he didn't want her to feel that this was some sort of a two-for-one deal. "You don't have to do that," he insisted.

"You didn't have to offer to watch Jonathan for me, or teach him—and me—a few of the basic commands," she countered.

Christopher could see that arguing with her was futile. She certainly didn't look stubborn, but she obviously was.

"Point taken," he allowed, "but this—" he gestured around "—is a lot more than just having a pet take up a little space."

"Potato, po*tat*o." She sniffed. "Those are my terms, take them or leave them."

He didn't quite comprehend the connection and said as much. "Not quite sure what you're getting at, but all right," he agreed, knowing when to surrender and when to dig in and fight. This was not the time for the latter. "I guess I could stand the help."

Lily smiled her approval at him. "Good, because I was going to help you whether you wanted me to or not," she told him.

"And just how were you going to do that?" Chris-

topher asked, curious. "You don't know where anything goes."

"Granted," she allowed. "But I'm good at making
educated guesses, and besides, I'm pretty sure you'd
break down eventually and tell me."

"Can we eat first?" Christopher suggested, nodding
at the pizza box, which was now on the coffee table,
awaiting their pleasure. "After all, the boxes aren't
going anywhere."

"True, but they also aren't going to unpack themselves," Lily countered.

"How about a compromise?" he asked.

Lily had always believed in compromise. And, in
any event, she didn't want the man thinking she was
some sort of a fanatic who picked up all the marbles
and went home if she couldn't have her way.

"Go ahead," she urged, "I'm listening."

"We each have a slice first, *then* we get started," he
suggested, shifting the box so that it seemed closer to
her. "I don't know about you, but I had a nonstop day
and I'm starving. If I don't eat something soon, I'm not
going to have enough energy to *open* a box, much less
put whatever's in the box away."

That just about described her day as well, she
thought. But before she could say as much, or agree
with him, her stomach rumbled, as if to remind her
that it was running on empty. She'd worked through
lunch, grabbing a handful of cherry tomatoes to try to
appease her hunger. Cherry tomatoes only went so far.

"I'll take that as a yes," Christopher concluded with
a satisfied grin. To cinch his argument, he raised the
lid on the pizza box and inhaled deeply. The aroma

was damn near seductive. "Right now, that smells almost as good to me as your pastries did the other day."

"Okay, one slice apiece and then we work. If you point me in the right direction, I'll get a couple of plates and napkins," she offered.

Christopher laughed. "Thanks, but it would probably take me more time to explain where to find them than it would take for me to get them myself." He began to cross to the kitchen, then abruptly stopped as one of the dogs sashayed around him. "Guard the pizza," he told Lily. "And look fierce," he added. "If either Leopold or Max detect the slightest weakness, they'll tag team you and get that box away from you before you even know what's going on."

She looked at him, utterly stunned. "Tag team?" Lily repeated. "You mean like in wrestling?"

That seemed rather unbelievable to her. After all, Christopher was talking about dogs, and while this was still pretty unfamiliar territory to her, she wasn't about to endow four-footed animals with a humanlike thought process.

He had to be pulling her leg.

But Christopher seemed dead serious. "Exactly like in wrestling." He looked rather surprised and then pleased that she was familiar with the term he'd used. "Don't let those faces fool you. They're a cunning duo."

"Apparently," she murmured.

She wasn't sure if she believed Christopher, but she focused her attention on the two Great Danes just to be on the safe side.

Meanwhile, Jonathan had gotten tired trying to get the best of the two older, larger dogs and had fallen back on the familiar. He had plopped down at her feet where he remained, lying there like a panting rug. He continued to stay there even after Christopher returned with a handful of napkins as well as a couple of plates.

The second Christopher offered her the first slice, Leopold and Max both raised their heads, their interests completely engaged.

"Down, boys," Christopher ordered. "You're not being polite to our guest." When the two dogs continued to stare at Lily's plate and drool, he said the command a second time, this time with more force.

Moving as one, the two Great Danes dropped their heads, sank down on the floor simultaneously and stretched out. Within seconds, their eyelids had drooped—along with their heads.

She could have sworn the two dogs had instantaneously fallen asleep.

Chapter Twelve

She stared at the two Great Danes for another few seconds. The sound of even breathing was evident. They really *were* asleep, she marveled.

"Nice trick," she said to Christopher, greatly impressed by the way his pets had responded to him. He had a gift, no two ways about it, she thought.

"Training," he corrected.

Lily supposed it was all in the way someone looked at it. But he did have a point. She could see how there would be no living with animals as large as these two dogs were if he hadn't succeeded in rigorously training them to respond to his commands.

"That, too," she allowed.

"Want another one?" he asked her.

Lily turned around to face him. She wasn't sure what the veterinarian was referring to. "Training trick?" she asked uncertainly.

He laughed. "No, pizza slice." He moved the opened box closer to her side of the coffee table. "You finished the slice I gave you, but there's still three quarters of a box to go."

"No, thank you, not right now." She had more than enough room for another slice, but she really wanted to make at least a slight dent in this box city that was invading his house. The aroma from the pizza teased her senses. She would have given in if she'd been less disciplined. "Although I can see the attraction," she admitted.

Christopher's eyes skimmed over her a little slower than they might have. "Yes, me, too."

Her mouth curved, silently accepting the compliment he was giving her. "I'm talking about the pizza," she told him pointedly.

"I know. Me, too," he replied whimsically. He still wasn't looking at the slices inside the pizza box.

Lily felt herself growing warmer, her mind filling with thoughts that had nothing to do with restoring order to his house, or eating pizza, or training unruly puppies. The way he watched her made her feel desirable; moreover, it made her imagination take flight.

Right, because you're so irresistible, just like veritable catnip to the man, the little voice in her head mocked.

Straighten up and fly right, she silently lectured. Out loud, she laid out terms that she felt would satisfy both of them.

"We can both have another slice after we each unpack two boxes," she told him. When he gave her a rather amused, dubious look, she amended her terms. "Okay, one box for you, two for me." Then, in case he thought she was saying she was faster than he was, she explained, "I've had practice at packing and un-packing."

He got started opening the large box next to the sofa. "You moved around often?"

She laughed softly, shaking her head. The house she lived in was the house she'd been born in. "Not even once."

For a second, he seemed slightly lost. "Then why—?"

"—did I say I've had practice?" She filled in the rest of his question and continued, "Because I have. I pack pastries before they're transported to their destination and once they get there, I have to unpack them, mak-ing sure that they make it to the table in perfect con-dition, the way the customer expected when they paid the catering bill. Making sure the pastries are displayed to their best advantage requires a delicate touch," she pointed out. "There's nothing worse-looking than a squashed or lopsided pastry or cake at a party."

"If they taste anywhere near as good as what I've sampled from your oven so far, I'd be willing to scrape them off the inside of a cardboard box just to be able to eat them."

She laughed. "That's very nice of you, but it doesn't change my point, which is that I can unpack things quickly, whereupon it looks as if you're willing to latch on to any excuse, any port in a storm no matter how flimsy it might be, just as long as you don't have to tackle what's inside those boxes."

"Busted," Christopher freely admitted, then in his defense, he added, "I'm pretty much the same way about groceries, which is why I don't have any and

I'm on a first-name basis with a lot of take-out places around here."

Pushing up her sleeves, Lily turned her attention to the closest large carton. "I wouldn't have pegged you as a procrastinator."

On the contrary, she would have said that he seemed like the type that tackled whatever was in front of him rather than putting it off till another time. Looks could be deceptive.

His were also very distracting, she couldn't help noticing.

"I guess that makes me a man of mystery—someone you *can't* read like an open book," he said, amusement highlighting his face.

"What that makes you," she corrected, "is a man who needs to be prodded. Now, do you have a utility knife—or if you don't, just a plain knife will do," she told him. She'd tried pulling the carton apart and the top just wouldn't give. "I just need something I can open the boxes with. If I keep trying to do it with my bare hands, I'm going to wind up breaking off all my nails in the process."

"I wouldn't want you to do that," he told her, going back to the kitchen to get a knife out of one of the drawers.

When he gave it to her, hilt first, she nodded toward the utensils that were in the drawer. "So you did put some things away."

He glanced over his shoulder, back at the drawer, which hadn't closed properly and had subsequently rolled back open again. He crossed to it to reclose it.

"Much as I'd like to take the credit," he answered, "no, I didn't."

"The drawer's full, and from what I could see those were all utensils in it. In other words, it's not just a junk drawer that you tossed things into as you came cross them. That's organization."

"No," he corrected, "that's my mother. Those were her utensils. After she died, I just couldn't get myself to throw any of her things away."

Not to mention the fact that hers had been a better quality than the ones he'd picked up when he'd lived off campus while attending school back East. When things had blown up on him so suddenly with Irene, he'd just told the movers to throw everything into boxes and move the lot to his mother's house in California.

She understood where he was coming from. But right now, the issue was a practical one of two things not being able to occupy the same space.

"There are always charities you can donate things to," she told him gently.

Christopher nodded. He knew she was right. "Soon—but not yet."

Lily didn't want him to think she was being in-sensitive—or pushy, especially not in this instance. "Actually, I understand exactly how you feel. When my mother passed away, I couldn't get myself to give anything of hers away, either. But after a while, I de-cided I was being selfish. My mother had a lot of nice things that still had a lot of life left in them. There were women out there who were—and are—needy, who could use one nice pair of shoes, or one nice dress, to lift their spirits, to maybe even turn them around and start them back toward a positive feeling of self-worth."

Lily went on talking as she methodically emptied

the first box, arranging its contents on the coffee table and the floor next to it.

"My mother was the type that liked helping people, even when she barely had anything herself. I know she would have wanted me to give her things away, so I picked a few special things to keep, things that really reminded me of her, and then I distributed the rest between a handful of charities. But it took me a long time before I could do that," she emphasized. "So I really do understand exactly what you're feeling."

Lily was coming to the bottom of the box and she felt that she had to comment on what she'd found while unpacking.

"You know, for a man who doesn't like to unpack, you certainly pack well."

Christopher thought of letting her comment go and just accepting it as a compliment. But not saying anything was practically like lying—or at least allowing a lie to be established. He couldn't do that, seeing as how she was really putting herself out for him—as well as the fact that he was giving serious thought to having a relationship with this unique woman.

"Not me," he told her. She looked at him in surprise. "It was the movers I hired, they did the packing for me. Unfortunately, while they obviously could pack extremely efficiently, they couldn't be bribed to unpack once they reached their destination."

"You actually tried to bribe them?" she asked, trying not to laugh at him.

"No," he admitted, "but looking back, I should have. I honestly didn't think that I would be putting it off as long as I have. But each day I found a reason not to get started—and Leopold and Max didn't seem to mind," he added, spreading the blame around. "I actually think they kind of like having all these boxes scattered throughout the house. For them it's like having their own private jungle gym."

This time she did laugh. "No offense, but I don't think dogs care about a jungle gym. In any case, even if they do, they're going to have to adjust," she informed him.

For the time being, she set the now-empty box to one side. She intended to break the carton down for easier transport and recycling later.

Christopher looked at her a little uncertainly. "Are you telling me that you intend to stay here until all these boxes are unpacked and taken apart?"

She couldn't tell if he was just surprised—or if the idea of her being here like that put him off. "No—but I do intend to keep coming back until they are."

Curiosity got the better of him. None of his old friends from high school had ever volunteered to help him conquer this cardboard kingdom of his. "Why would you do that?"

There was no hesitation on her part. "Call it repaying one favor with another—besides, my mother taught me to never leave something half-done. The job's done when the job's done," she told the veterinarian, reciting an old axiom.

She'd amused him—again. "That sounds like something out of Yogi Berra's playbook," he said, referring to the famous Yankees catcher.

The smile she gave him told Christopher that she was familiar with baseball history. Something else they had in common, he couldn't help thinking.

"Wise man, Yogi Berra," Lily commented with a smile as she went back to work.

By the end of the evening, they had managed to unpack a total of five boxes and they had put away the contents of three of them—not to mention all but polishing off the pizza he had ordered. There were only two slices left, which Christopher earmarked for his breakfast for the following morning.

Tired, Lily rotated her shoulders to loosen them a little.

"Well, I've got an early day tomorrow," she told Christopher, "so I'd better be going home."

He wanted to ask her to stay a little longer. Not to unpack, but just to talk.

Just to *be*.

He found that he liked Lily's company, liked her sense of humor and her determination, as well. Liked, too, the way her presence seemed to fill up his house far more than the towering boxes she had them tackling ever had.

But asking her to stay when she had to be up early would be selfish of him. So he let the moment pass—except to voice his thanks for her help as he walked her and Jonathan to the door.

"You know, this has to be one of the most unique evenings I've ever spent," he confessed, then added, "I enjoyed it."

The dimpled smile on his face seemed to work its way into every single nook and corner of her being. Lily returned his smile and replied, "So did I."

He wanted to be sure that, despite what she'd said, having her work like this, putting his things away, wasn't going to ultimately scare her off. So he asked, "And you'll be dropping Jonny off at the animal hospital tomorrow?"

She wanted to, but there was a problem. "I've got to be at work at seven," she told him, knowing the clinic opened at eight.

If she needed to leave the dog at seven, then he was going to be there at seven. He found himself *wanting* to be there for her. "Funny, so do I."

"No, you don't," she countered, seeing through his lie. She didn't want to put him out and he'd already been so helpful to her.

He pretended to narrow his eyes, giving her a reproving look. "It's not nice to call your pet's doctor a liar."

Her heart felt as if it was under assault. Her mouth curved again as she shook her head. "I'm not calling you a liar—" Then, whimsically, she made a suggestion. "How about a stretcher of truth?"

"I'll take that under consideration," he told her. His tone changed as he told her fondly, "Now go home and get some sleep."

That was the plan. Whether or not it worked was going to be another story, she thought, looking at Christopher. "Thanks for the pizza."

"Thanks for the help," he countered. "And for the kick in the pants."

That sounded so callous when he said it that way. "I didn't kick, I prodded," she amended politely.

He laughed as he inclined his head, playing along. "I stand corrected." Reaching the door, he paused, his brain engaged in a verbal tennis match. He decided to leave the decision up to her—sort of.

"Lily—"

There was something in his voice that put her on alert. "Yes?"

His eyes held hers for a full moment before Christopher put his question to her. "Would you mind if I kissed you?"

This time, the smile she offered began in her eyes. "Actually," Lily admitted, "I think I'd mind if you didn't."

"I definitely wouldn't want that," Christopher confessed as he framed her face with his hands. The next moment he brought his lips down to hers.

It began lightly, politely, but almost instantly took on a life and breadth of its own, escalating quickly. Along with that escalation, it brought with it a whole host of emotions.

She didn't quite recall wrapping her arms around Christopher's neck, didn't remember, once anchored to him this way, tilting her body into his. What she did remember was the wild burst of energy that seemed to spring out of nowhere and wrapped itself around her tightly for the duration of that intense kiss.

Lily's mouth tasted of every forbidden fruit he'd ever fantasized about. It made him want more.

Made him want her.

He struggled to hold himself in check, to only go so far and no further. It was far from easy, but he was not about to pay this woman back for her help, for her providing him with his first decent evening since his breakup with Irene, for giving him his first shot at feeling *human* since Irene had taken a two-by-four to his life—and his pride—he was not going to pay her back for all that by overpowering Lily and forcing himself on her.

So, with a wave of what he felt was close to super-human control, Christopher forced himself to back away from what could have easily become his with just the right moves.

He wasn't about "moves," he reminded himself, he was about sincerity, no matter *what* his body was attempting to dictate to him.

Drawing back, he paused to take a couple of discreet, very deep breaths, doing his best to regulate the timbre of his voice.

"Thank you again," he murmured.

She knew he wasn't thanking her for helping him to unpack those few boxes. She struggled to stifle the blush that wanted so badly to take root. But she didn't seem to have a say in that. Her body seemed to be on its own timetable, one that had little to do with anything she might have dictated.

After a beat, Lily cleared her throat, managed to murmur something that sounded like "Don't mention it," and then left quickly with her puppy.

She wasn't sure just how long it had taken for her heartbeat to settle down and return to normal. All she was aware of was that it had remained rather erratic for the entire trip home, and even for a few minutes after she'd walked into her house.

She was also aware of the happy glow that had taken hold of her.

This, she felt rather certain, was the very first leg of the journey that ultimately led to genuine affection. Lily stubbornly refused to use the *L* word to describe what she might wind up achieving since she felt if she did, she might just jinx what was happening.

Deep down, though she wasn't a superstitious person by nature, she was afraid that thinking about falling in love with this man would almost assuredly guarantee that there would be no happily ever after waiting for her at the finish line.

Besides, she hardy knew anything about the man except that he hated unpacking—and he had a killer smile. The really safe, smart thing to do, Lily told herself as she unlocked the front door and Jonathan pushed the door opened with his shoulder, walking right in, would be for her to find Jonathan another veterinarian.

If she went that route, it would guarantee that she would have no entanglements with the man whose house she'd just left, no further temptation to wander down the wrong road someday soon.

Oh, who are you kidding? she scolded herself.

She had never been one to automatically opt for doing things the "smart way," especially if that "smart way" promised just more of the same.

More dullness, more playing it safe.

And that in turn meant that there wouldn't be anything to light up her life. Nothing would cause her fingertips to tingle and her imagination to take flight, going to places she would have never admitted to yearning for, at least not out loud.

"You continue torturing yourself like this and you are not going to get any sleep no matter what you try. Turn off your brain, change into your pj's and for God's sake, get some rest before you wind up dropping from exhaustion."

Easier said than done.

Oh, she could certainly change into her pajamas and crawl into bed. The next-to-impossible part of the equation was the part about turning off her brain.

Her brain, it seemed, wanted only to vividly relive that last kiss and play it over and over again in her mind's eye, heightening every last nuance to its uppermost limit.

She was doomed and she knew it.

Resigned, Lily went up the stairs to her bedroom, her four-footed black shadow following right behind her, barking happily.

Chapter Thirteen

Christopher knew it would make a difference, but until the job was almost completed, he hadn't realized just how *much* of a difference the undertaking would actually make.

Each time he looked around, the amount of space surprised him all over again. Without fully being conscious of it, he'd gotten accustomed to weaving his way in and out between the boxes, accepting the clutter that existed as a given. With Lily insisting on helping him unpack the countless boxes, large and small, that had been here for months, the house gradually returned to looking like the place he'd known during his childhood, growing up with a single mom. Lily had not only gotten him to organize and clear away the physical clutter, but through doing that he had also wound up clearing away some emotional clutter, as well.

Without boxes being everywhere he turned, Christopher felt as if his ability to think clearly had vastly improved, allowing him to finally move forward in his private life.

It was almost as if his brain was like a hard drive that had been defragmented. The analogy wasn't his. Lily had tossed the comparison his way when he'd commented that he felt less oppressed, more able to think these past few days. He thought her analogy seemed to hit the nail right on the head.

As they worked together, he discovered that Lily had an uncanny ability to simplify things. She seemed to see into his very soul.

Without discussing it or even being fully conscious of it, he and Lily had settled into a routine that was beneficial to both of them. Weekday mornings she would swing by with Jonathan, dropping the Labrador off at the animal hospital, and then in the evenings she would collect her pet and then follow Christopher to his home. Once there they would both tackle emptying out and breaking down at least one of the boxes, if not more.

They also ate dinner together, usually one she had prepared in his kitchen. It was just something she had gotten into the habit of doing. While he continued to tell her that she really didn't have to go out of her way like this, Christopher made no secret of his enjoyment of each and every meal she prepared.

As much as he appreciated her help de-cluttering his house and looked forward to exhibits of her stellar culinary abilities, what he looked forward to most of all were the conversations they had. Each evening while they worked and ate, they talked and got to know one another a little better than before.

It definitely made Christopher anticipate each evening.

Oh, he loved being a veterinarian, loved being able to improve the lives of almost all the animals who were brought to his hospital.

He was lucky enough to treat a larger variety of pets than most, everything from mice, hamsters and rabbits to dogs and cats and birds, as well as several other types of pets who fell somewhere in between. He couldn't remember a time when he hadn't wanted to be a veterinarian, and if he hadn't become one he honestly didn't know what he would be doing these days.

But Lily, well, she represented a completely different path in his life, a path he was both familiar with in a distant, cursory fashion, and one different enough for him to feel that he hadn't actually traveled it before.

She very quickly had become an integral part of his life. Being around her made him feel alive, with an endless font of possibilities before him. It was akin to being brought back from the dead after having attended his own funeral. He'd never thought he could feel like this again—and it was all because of Lily.

"We're almost done, you know," Lily said one evening, pointing out what she knew was the obvious. But it felt good to say it nonetheless. "There are just a few boxes left. When they're gone, I really won't have a reason to stop by here after work each night." She held her breath, waiting to see if Christopher would express regret or relief over what she'd just said.

His answer more than pleased her—and put her mind at ease. "I could try rustling up some more boxes, maybe steal some from the local UPS office or from FedEx, or the post office on Murphy if all else fails."

She laughed at the very thought of his contemplating hijacking boxes. He was nothing if not exceedingly upstanding. "It's not the same thing."

He stopped working and looked at Lily seriously. She had become part of his life so quickly that it all but took his breath away.

Just like she did.

"I'd still do it if it meant that it would keep you coming over every evening. Besides, as selfish as this might sound, you've gotten me hooked on your cooking. I find myself expecting it by the end of the day," he freely admitted. "You wouldn't want to deprive me of it, now, would you?"

She turned away from the box she'd almost finished emptying and gazed at him, a hint of a pleased smile playing on her lips. "Just so I'm clear on this, let me get this straight. You want me to keep coming over so I can continue unpacking your boxes and cooking your dinner, is that right?"

"What I want," he told her, crossing over to Lily and taking the book that she'd just removed from the last box out of her hands, "is to continue having *you* to look forward to each evening."

His eyes on hers, Christopher let the book he'd just taken out of her hands fall to the floor.

He realized that he was risking a great deal, crawling out on a limb that had no safety net beneath it. But if he didn't, if he didn't *say* something, he ran the very real risk of losing her, of having her just walk away from his life.

This, he knew, was a crossroads for them, for although they had shared an occasional heated moment, an occasional kiss, they had each always returned to their corners, respectful of the other's barriers and limits. They pushed no boundaries, leaving envelopes exactly where they lay.

Risk nothing, gain nothing.

Or, in this case, Christopher thought, risk nothing, lose everything.

He didn't want to lose everything.

"I'd still be stopping by the animal hospital to pick up Jonathan," Lily reminded him. "That is, if, once we're finished here, you'd still be willing to have me drop him off with you in the morning."

"Sure, that goes without saying," he assured her. Jonathan barked as if he knew he was being talked about, but Christopher continued focusing on her. "Everyone looks forward to having Jonny around during the day. But that still leaves a large chunk of my evening empty. I'm not sure I'd know how to deal with that," he told her in a voice that had become hardly louder than a whisper.

As she listened, giving him her undivided attention, that whisper seemed to feather along her lips, softly seducing her, causing havoc to every single nerve ending within her body.

"Why don't we talk about it later?" Christopher suggested in between light, arousing passes along her lips.

"I know what you're doing," she said. It was an effort for her to think straight. "You're just trying to get me to stop unpacking the last boxes."

She saw his mouth curve in amusement, *felt* his smile seeping into her soul.

"I always said you were a very smart lady," Christopher told her.

"And you are exceedingly tricky. Lucky I majored in seeing through tricky," she quipped.

"Maybe lucky for you, not so much me," he told her in a low, unsettling voice.

He was still playing his ace card, Lily thought. Still managing to reduce her to a pliable, warmed-over puddle. And she'd discovered something just now, in this moment of truth. Christopher wasn't just hard to resist. When he got going, moving full steam ahead, the man was damn near *impossible* to resist.

Even so, she did her best to try.

Her best wasn't good enough.

Gladly taking the excuse that Christopher had so willingly handed her, she completely abandoned the box she'd been emptying, leaving it to be tackled on some other day. She certainly wasn't up to doing that this evening.

Tonight had suddenly become earmarked for something else entirely. Tonight she was finally going to give in to all the demands that had been mounting within her, all the demands that were vibrating within her.

She had given herself endless pep talks against taking the step she was contemplating, mentally listing all the reasons she would regret crossing this final line in the sand. The line separating flirtation from something a great deal more serious.

And possibly a great deal more fulfilling.

Commitment and, yes, possibly even love were on the other side of that line.

But just because she was willing to cross that line,

Lily reminded herself, that did not necessarily mean that he did or would.

Even if Christopher said it, said that he *wanted* to cross the line and made a show of embracing both concepts—commitment *and* love—that wouldn't really make it a reality. She wasn't naive enough to believe that just because someone said something meant that there had to be even an iota of truth to it.

That was the part where a leap of faith would need to come in.

She knew that. Logically, she knew that. But right now, logic had been left standing somewhere at a door far away. She would have to deal with this later, one way or another.

Right now, at this burning moment in time, Lily realized that what she wanted, what she *needed,* was to have him make her feel wanted, make her feel that she was special to him.

Never mind whether or not it was true. She would pretend it was true.

And maybe, just maybe, if wishing hard enough could make it so, it *would* be true. But again, that was a struggle, a battle to be undertaken later.

Right now, every fiber of her being wanted to be made love to—make love with—Christopher.

So rather than resist, or coyly move just out of his reach, gravitating toward another excuse, another roadblock to get in the way of what she knew they both wanted, Lily remained in his arms, kissed him back the way he had kissed her and, just like that, effectively brought down every single barrier, every makeshift fence, every concrete wall they had each put up to protect the most frail thing they each possessed: their hearts.

This was different, Christopher realized. She wasn't kissing him back with feeling, she was kissing him back with fire. He could feel the passion igniting, could feel it being passed back and forth between them and growing sharply in intensity by the nanosecond.

He kissed Lily over and over again and with each kiss he only craved more. He made love to her with his mouth, first to her lips, then to her throat, sliding down to the tender hollow between her breasts.

Her moan only served to inflame him more. It increased the tempo, inciting a riot right there within his veins.

Christopher was afraid of letting loose. And equally afraid not to.

To contain this amount of passion would bring about his own self-destruction. Not someday but before the evening's end.

Her hands passed over his chest, possessing him even before her fingertips dove beneath his shirt, sliding along the hard ridges of his pectorals, hardening him at the same time that she was reducing him to a mass of fluid flames and desires.

He had to hold back to keep from ripping off her clothes. But even as he tried to keep himself in check, he felt Lily's quick, urgent movements all but tearing away his shirt and slacks.

It was the proverbial straw, unleashing the passionate creature caged within.

His hands, sturdy and capable yet so gentle, were everywhere, touching, caressing, possessing.

Worshipping.

He just couldn't seem to get enough of her. He felt himself feeding on her softness; feeding on her frenzy as if it comprised the very substance of his existence.

As if Lily and only Lily could sustain his very life force.

Christopher was making her crazy, playing her body as if it was a highly tuned musical instrument that would only—*could* only—sing for him, because only he knew just how to unlock the melody that existed just beneath the surface.

Lily ached to feel his touch—to feel *him* along her body.

She arched her back, pressing herself against him as he made the fire inside of her rise to greater and greater heights.

There hadn't been all that many lovers and she knew she wasn't exactly all that experienced before tonight, but Lily honestly thought that she'd been to the table before. It was only now that she realized she had only had her nose pressed up against the glass window, aware of the existence of these sensations, but never really *feeling* any of them.

Certainly not like this.

She felt things now, responded to things now. Did things now, things that had never even crossed her mind to consider doing before tonight.

But suddenly, she wanted to pleasure this man who had utterly lit up her entire world. She wanted to give him back a little in kind of what he had so generously given her.

With the feel of his breath trailing along the more sensitive areas of her skin still incredibly, indelibly fresh along her body, Lily arched and wrapped her legs around his torso, teasing him, urging him to cross the final line.

To form the final union.

Her body urgently moving beneath his, Christopher discovered that he hadn't the strength to hold off any longer. His goal had been to bring her up and over to a climax a handful of times before he claimed the irresistible, but he was only so strong, could only hold out for so long and no more.

That time was now.

With a moan that echoed of surrender, Christopher proceeded to take what she so willingly offered him. Shifting seductively, Lily opened for him.

His mouth sealed to hers and, balancing his weight as best he could, he entered her.

Her sharp intake of breath almost drove him over the brink. At the last moment, he did his best to be gentle, to rein himself in before the ultimate ride took hold and control was all but yanked away from him, no matter how good his intentions.

The more she moved, the more he wanted her.

Wanting her became his only reality.

His heart pounding hard, Christopher stepped up his pace until the ride became dizzying for both of them.

By the end, just before the heat exploded, embracing them fiercely a beat before the inevitable descent began, he felt confident that he had been granted every wish he'd ever made in life.

The feeling was so intense, he tightened his arms around her to the point that he almost found himself merging with her very flesh.

Somehow, they remained two very distinct, if two very exhausted people. Two people clinging to one another, forming their own human life raft in the rough sea of reality as it gradually descended upon them and came back into focus.

When Christopher could finally draw enough air into his lungs to enable him to form a sentence, albeit a softly worded one, he kissed the top of her head and said, "I am definitely hijacking a moving van and having more boxes delivered."

She laughed and her warm breath both tickled him and somehow managed to begin to arouse him again. He didn't understand how that was possible, but there was a magic to this woman that seemed to make all things possible.

After all, he had been so sure, after what Irene had done to him, that he could never feel again, never *want* to feel again, and yet here he was, feeling and grateful to be doing it.

"I think," she said as she lay her head on his chest, "that we've gotten past that stage—needing boxes as an excuse."

Christopher managed to kiss the top of her head again before he fell back, almost exhausted by the effort as well as insanely happy.

"Can't argue with that," he said, the words straggling out one after the other in an erratic fashion. "Even if I wanted to," he added, "I can't argue. Not enough air in my lungs to argue and win."

He felt her smile against his chest. "Then I win by default."

They both laughed at the absurd way that sounded. And they laughed mainly because just hearing the sound of laughter felt so good and so satisfying, as well as oddly soothing at the same time.

Christopher's arms tightened around her.

Feeling Lily's heart beat against his felt as if it was the answer to everything that was important in his life.

He knew that he had never been happier than right at this very moment.

Chapter Fourteen

Lily very quickly came to the conclusion that there really was no graceful way to go from making mind-blowing love with a man to getting dressed and slipping back into the everyday world that she had temporarily stepped away from.

It would have been a great deal easier to get dressed and make her getaway if Christopher had been asleep. But the man who had lit up her entire world, complete with skyrockets and fireworks, was lying right beside her and he was very much awake.

Even if he was asleep, there was still the small matter of actually making a soundless getaway with her Labrador in tow *and* getting by Christopher's two Great Danes, Leopold and Max. She'd made friends with them over the past few weeks so she was fairly confident that the dogs wouldn't immediately begin barking the moment she stirred. But she had a feeling that they wouldn't turn into two docile statues, silently watching her slip out of the house with Jonathan in her arms.

Any attempt to see if she was right went up in smoke the very next moment.

"Going somewhere?" Christopher asked as she tried to sit up on the sofa, ready to begin the taxing hunt for her clothes—*any* of her clothes.

He slipped his arm around her waist, firmly holding her in place as he waited for her to come up with an answer.

"I thought I'd finish tidying up the family room, break down the empty boxes we left behind, little things like that," she told him innocently.

"In the nude?" Christopher sounded both amused and intrigued. "Glad I didn't doze off like you did. This I have to see."

She looked at him over her shoulder and protested, "I didn't doze off."

"Yes, you did, but that's okay," he told her. "It was only for a few minutes." He drew her in a little closer, his arm still around her waist. "Besides, you look cute when you sleep. Your face gets all soft."

Lily turned her body toward him and gazed down at his face. "As opposed to what? Being rock hard when I'm awake?"

"Not rock hard, but let's just say…guarded," he concluded, finally deciding upon a word. Once he said it out loud, it seemed to fit perfectly. "You know, kind of like a night watchman at an art museum who's afraid someone's going to steal a painting the second he lets his guard down."

Lily frowned. "Not exactly a very romantic image," she commented.

"But an accurate one," he pointed out. His intention hadn't been to insult her or scare her away. He was just being observant. "You don't have to go, you know."

Oh, yes I do. I can't think around you, especially after this.

"I know," she said out loud. "But I'm thinking that a little space between us might not be a bad thing, so I can get my bearings."

He wasn't about to keep her against her will if it came down to that, but he wasn't going to just give up without a word, either.

"A GPS can give you the exact latitude and longitude, but it can't give you a secure feeling. That kind of thing only happens between people," he told Lily, lightly brushing her hair away from her face.

She felt herself tensing. Reacting. "Don't do that," she told him, moving her head back, away from him. "I can't think when you do that."

"Good, I was hoping you'd say that."

Lying back against the sofa again, Christopher pulled her down to him. Before she could make a half-hearted protest, his lips brushed hers.

In less than a moment, she lost the desire to speak, as well. He had relit her fire and they began making love all over again.

There were still a few boxes left scattered around his house. It was a definite improvement over the first time she'd walked into the older home, but the fact that there were any left at all bothered her.

But each time she thought they were going to spend

a quiet evening going through the last of moving cartons, something came up. The first time he'd had another emergency surgery to perform, this time on a mixed-breed dog that had been left on the animal shelter's doorstep. The poor dog had been more dead than alive and, he'd explained to Lily, he was one of the vets who volunteered their services at the shelter. He couldn't find it in his heart to say no when they called. One look at the sad mutt—a photo had been sent to his smart phone—and neither could Lily.

She'd insisted on coming with him to help in any way she could. As sometimes happened, she had made extra pastries for the event that Theresa's company had been catering that day, and Lily brought some of the overage with her to share with Christopher and the other volunteers who were at the shelter.

In the end, the surgery had been a success—and so had her pastries.

"I think they want to permanently adopt you," he told Lily as they left the shelter several hours later. He smiled at her, lingering in the all-but-deserted parking lot. "Those pastries you brought with you were certainly a hit. Thanks."

She looked at him a bit uncertainly. "For what?"

"For coming along. For being so understanding. For being you." He took her into his arms, something he had gotten very used to doing. "It's pretty late, but we can curl up in front of the TV and not pay attention to whatever's on cable. I can order in."

"You need your rest," she told him, amused.

He kissed the top of her head. "What makes you think I won't be resting?"

Amusement highlighted her face. "I'm beginning to know you."

"Damn, foiled again. I'll make it up to you tomorrow," he promised.

She paused for a moment, tilted her head back and, grabbing the front of his shirt, pulled him down slightly to her level. Lily pressed her lips against his, kissing him with feeling.

Before either of them could get carried away, she moved her head back and told him, "There's nothing to make up for. I like watching you come to the rescue like that. You're like a knight in shining armor, except that instead of a lance, you're wielding a scalpel." Stepping away from him, she unlocked her car. The second she opened up the rear passenger door, Jonathan bounded inside. "Now go home."

"Yes, ma'am," he answered obediently, then repeated, "Tomorrow."

"Tomorrow," she echoed.

Despite occasional detours like that, she had expected that they would be back on track the next evening, spending it at his place, unpacking the last of the boxes that were upstairs in his bedroom. Dinner would consist of something she'd prepared.

But when Christopher closed up the hospital for the evening, he informed her that he had a surprise for her.

"What kind of surprise?" she asked suspiciously.

"The kind you'll find out about when we get there," he said mysteriously.

"We're going somewhere?"

"Good deduction," he applauded.

"Shouldn't we drop Jonathan off first?"

"No. He's coming along with us."

"Then we're not going out to eat?" That would have been her first guess at the kind of surprise he was taking her to.

Instead of answering, he merely smiled at her and told her to follow him.

She was intrigued. He had succeeded in capturing her complete attention.

"This is a restaurant," she noted when, fifteen minutes later, she had pulled her vehicle up next to his in a semicrowded parking lot. She was standing beside her car, looking at the squat building that was obviously Christopher's intended destination.

"It is," he confirmed cheerfully.

"We can't leave Jonathan in the car while we eat."

"We're not going to," he informed her, taking the leash from her hand.

"But—"

"Ruff's is a restaurant where people can go to dine out with their pets," he told her. "I thought you might get a kick out of it.

She didn't get a kick out of it, she *loved* it and told him as much over dinner, and continued to do so when they got back to his place.

"How did you find it?" she asked.

"One of my patients' owners opened it up not too long ago. I thought it was an idea whose time has come. I'm one of the investors," he confided to her.

"Really?" The idea excited her—just as the man did, she thought as she felt him trail his fingertips along the hollow of her throat.

"Really," he confirmed. "I'd never lie to a beautiful woman."

"But I'm the only one in the room."

He laughed. "Fishing for compliments, are we?"

She put her hand to her breast. "Me?"

"You," he said, nipping her lower lip.

That was the last of the conversation for quite a while.

"Who's this?" Lily asked, pulling a framed photograph out of the last carton that was still only semi-unpacked in his bedroom.

Time had gotten away from her and she'd wound up spending the night. Which meant she needed to hurry getting dressed so she could swing by her place and get a fresh change of clothing before proceeding on to work.

They had already decided, sometime during the night, that Jonathan would remain here and Christopher would take the dog with him when he went in to the animal hospital.

The framed photograph—Christopher posing with an aristocratic-looking brunette, his arm around her waist in the exact same fashion that it had been around hers that first time she'd tried to slip out of his bed— had all but fallen at her feet when she'd bumped into the open box. It had fallen over, spilling out its contents. The framed photograph was the first thing she saw.

"Who's who?" Christopher asked, preoccupied.

He was searching the immediate area for his keys. He assumed they had fallen somewhere as he and Lily had made love last night. Rather than settling into a certain predictability, their lovemaking only seemed to get better each time.

Instead of answering, she turned toward Christopher holding up the framed photograph. "This woman you've got your arm around," she told him. Even as the words came out, she had a sinking feeling she wasn't going to like his answer.

Christopher's mind went temporarily blank as he saw the frame she had in her hands. "Where did you get that?" he asked, his throat drier than he could ever recall it being.

"It fell out of that box when I accidentally knocked it over," she told him, nodding her head toward the carton that was still on in its side. "Who is she, Chris?" Lily repeated. With each word, the deadness inside of her seemed to grow a little larger, a little more threatening. "She has to be someone because you wouldn't have packed up this photograph if she wasn't."

"I didn't do any of the packing," he reminded her. "The movers did."

The point was that it had been there, at his residence, for them to pack. The fact that he was being evasive right now just made her more anxious.

"Well, it has to be yours," she insisted. "The movers wouldn't have packed up a stranger's things and put them into your moving van—besides, you're *in* the picture and that's your arm around her waist." Each word tasted more bitter than the last. "Who *is* she, Chris?" Lily asked for a third time, growing impatient. It wasn't as if they didn't both have pasts, but she didn't like the idea of not knowing enough about him—and his having secrets.

"She's nobody," he told her, taking the frame out of her hand and tossing it facedown on his rumpled bed.

Lily squared her shoulders defiantly. "If she was nobody, you would have said that right away. You don't take a picture with nobody and then have it framed," she pointed out. "Why won't you tell me who she is?"

Christopher blew out a breath. He'd honestly thought he'd thrown that photograph—all the photographs of her—out. "Because she doesn't matter anymore."

Lily heard what wasn't being said. "But she did once, right?"

"Once," he admitted because to say otherwise would really be lying.

Lily's voice became very quiet. "How much did she matter?"

Because he knew he had to, Christopher gave her the briefest summary of the time he had spent with Irene. "Her name was Irene Masterson and we were engaged—but we're not anymore," he emphasized. "We haven't been for three months."

Three months. The words echoed in her brain. She had him on the rebound. There was no other way to interpret this. She was a filler, a placeholder until he got his act together. How could she have been so stupid as to think this was going somewhere? Things didn't go anywhere except into some dark abyss.

For a moment, Lily stared at him, speechless. She felt her very fragile world shattering and crumbling. "And you didn't think that was important enough to tell me?"

He told her the only thing he could in his own defense. "The topic never came up."

Was he saying it was her fault because she hadn't interrogated him?

"Maybe it should have," she countered, feeling hurt beyond words. "Preferably before things got too hot and heavy between us." At the last moment, she had stopped herself from saying "serious between us" because it wasn't. How could it be if he had kept something so important from her? She'd been deluding herself about his feelings for her. It was painfully obvious now that she had read far too much into ther relationship. There wasn't a "relationship," it was just a matter of killing time for him, nothing more.

"I don't remember a single place where I could have segued into that. When was I supposed to say something?" he asked. "Just before we came together? 'Excuse me, Lily, but in the interest of full disclosure, I think you should know that I had a serious girlfriend for a few years and we were engaged for five months.'"

Five months. The woman in the photograph had had a claim on him for five months—longer than they had known each other. Plus, it had only ended recently, which made her presence in his life shaky at best. The very thought twisted in her stomach, stealing the air out of her lungs.

"Yes," she retorted. "You should have told me, should have said something."

Trying to get hold of herself, Lily took a deep breath.

This was her fault, not his. Her fault because she'd given in to the longing, the loneliness she'd felt, thinking that she'd finally found a steady, decent man, someone she could love and go through life with. But Christopher wasn't the guy. He couldn't be with what he'd just gone through. She didn't want to be the girl who picked up other people's messes, a placeholder while the injured party healed.

Her voice was emotionless as she said, "Why aren't you still engaged?"

Christopher lifted a shoulder and let it fall in a careless shrug. "We wanted different things. She wanted me to change, to be someone else, someone who fit into her blue-blooded world. I didn't want to change."

Lily was struggling to understand, to come to grips with what she'd just stumbled across. Trying to tell herself that it didn't matter when every fiber of her being told her that it did.

"Did the engagement just disintegrate on its own?" she asked.

What could he say to make this right? To fix what he seemed to have broken? "It probably would have in time."

Her eyes held his. "But?"

He had no choice. He had to tell her the truth and pray that he wasn't going to regret it. "But with everything going on, losing my mother, I just wanted to get away and be done with it."

Her expression gave him no indication what she was thinking. "So you broke it off?"

Christopher nodded. "Yes."

She needed to get this absolutely straight in her mind. "You made a commitment to someone you loved and then you broke it off?" she pressed.

He wanted to deny it, to deny that he had ever loved Irene. But he *had* loved her, and if he lied about it he knew it would backfire on him, if not now then someday. That damage would be irreparable.

"Yes."

The sadness that washed over her with that single word was almost overwhelming. She couldn't stay here any longer, not without breaking down. "I have to go," she said abruptly. "Jonathan!" she called, her voice growing edgy. "Jonathan, come!"

After a moment, the Labrador appeared at the bottom of the stairs, barking at her. Lily practically ran down the stairs. Not wanting to waste time looking for his leash, she grabbed the dog's collar and as quickly as possible guided him toward the front door.

Christopher flew down the stairs right behind her. "Wait, I thought we agreed that I'd take him to the animal hospital for you this morning."

Lily didn't even turn around. "There's no need. He's coming with me."

"Lily—" Her name echoed of all the hurt, the concern that was ricocheting through him.

"I've change my mind, okay?" she snapped, afraid that she would start to cry at any second. She had to get out of there before it happened. "You changed yours, right? Why can't I change mine?"

Wanting to sweep her into his arms, to hold her against him until she calmed down, Christopher took a step back instead. His instincts told him not to press. "Sure, you can change your mind," he told her quietly. "Will I still see you tonight?"

"I don't think that's a good idea," she told him crisply.

Lily found she had to all but drag Jonathan away— the Labrador seemed reluctant to leave both his canine friends and the man who had treated him so nicely. When he resisted, Lily pulled his collar harder, said his name in a very authoritative voice followed by a command that Christopher had taught her. After a second, Jonathan followed her.

The training had worked out well, she thought, fighting back tears as she crossed the threshold. The trainer, however, had not.

"Lily," Christopher called after her. "I don't want you to leave."

It took a great deal for him to put himself out there like that after he had promised himself not to even think about having a relationship with a woman until he had gotten over his grieving period. Telling himself that his mother would have really liked Lily hadn't exactly tipped the scales in Lily's favor—but it hadn't hurt, either.

"Now," she said, aiming the words over her shoulder as she hurried to her car. "You don't want me to leave *now*. But you'll change your mind soon enough," she said between clenched teeth. She had to clench them or risk beginning to sob.

Served her right for allowing herself to connect with a man so quickly. Lily could feel tears aching in her throat.

Two weeks passed.

Two weeks that moved with the torturous pace of a crippled turtle. Every minute of every day seemed to register as time dragged itself from one end of the day to the other. He felt as if he was going crazy. His work, rather than being his haven, became his trial instead.

He had trouble concentrating.

He tried to move on, he really did. Following his breakup with Irene, after the initial hurt subsided and after he stopped feeling as if he'd been a colossal fool for missing all the signs that had been right there in front of him, Christopher had actually experienced a sense of relief. The kind of relief survivors experienced after learning that they had just narrowly managed to dodge a bullet. The young woman he had thought he had fallen in love with wouldn't have been the woman that he was supposed to end up marrying. Avoiding that was the part where the relief came in.

But in this case, with Lily, there was no sense of relief. There was only a sense of loss, a sense that something very special had somehow managed to slip right through his fingers and he was never going to be able to recover what he had lost.

Consequently, life had progressively become darker for him. It felt as if the light had gone out of his world and he had no way to turn it back on. Resigned to this new, grimmer view of life, he found his whole demeanor changing.

Theresa had alerted her that something was definitely up. She'd said that Lily had become very quiet and withdrawn these past two weeks and that the young woman had taken to bringing the puppy to work with her instead of leaving Jonathan with Christopher. But atypically, Theresa had added, Lily wasn't talking. The pastry chef had told her that everything was "fine" every time she'd asked if something was wrong.

Maizie decided to find out some things for herself.

Which was why she popped into the animal clinic the following Tuesday, when things had slowed down in her own real estate office.

She came armed with one of Cecilia's remaining puppies, telling the receptionist that she had recently acquired this pet and was going to give it to her grand-daughter as a gift. Erika had managed to fit her in between scheduled appointments.

"Hi," Maizie said cheerfully, popping into the last exam room where she'd been told she'd find the object of her visit. "Your receptionist—lovely girl, Erika," she commented before continuing, "said you were back here and that it was all right for me to bring Walter to you. I hope you don't mind my just dropping by. But Walter's going to be a gift for my granddaughter and I just want to be sure he's healthy before I give him to her," she said.

Christopher stared at the puppy. It looked almost exactly like Jonathan. But it couldn't be—could it?

"Where did you get him?" he asked Maizie.

"I know a breeder up north, around Santa Barbara," Maizie replied innocently. "Why do you ask?"

Christopher tried to sound casual as he explained, but just the thought of Lily put longing in his voice. "Someone I know has a dog just like that. She said he just turned up on her doorstep a couple of months ago."

Maizie pretended to take the story in stride. "I hear that Labradors are popular these days because they're so friendly. That's why I got one for my granddaughter." She looked closely at Christopher as he proceeded to examine the puppy. "Is something wrong, dear?"

"The puppy seems to be fine," he said as he continued with his exam.

"I was talking about you, Christopher," Maizie said gently.

He shrugged, wishing the woman would just focus on the puppy she'd brought in and not ask him any personal questions. He couldn't deal with them right now.

He'd left numerous messages on Lily's phone. She hadn't called back once. When he went by her house, there were never any lights on and she didn't answer the door when he rang the bell.

"I'm fine," he told Maizie again.

Maizie placed her hand on his shoulder—she had to reach up a little in order to do it. "You know, Christopher, I feel that I owe it to your mother to tell you that as an actor, you're not very convincing. What's bothering you?" she asked. "I might not be able to help, but I can certainly give you a sympathetic ear."

He didn't want to talk about it. Concluding his exam, he looked at her. "Walter's very healthy. And as for me... Mrs. Connors, I know you mean well—"

Maizie took the puppy off the exam table and placed him on the floor. "You can call me Maizie at this point and hell, yes, I mean well." Her eyes locked with the young veterinarian's. "When my daughter looked like you do right now, it was because something in her relationship with the man she eventually married— wonderful son-in-law, by the way—had gone wrong. Now, out with it. You need an impartial third party to tell you if you're overreacting or if you should give up—and since your mother's not here to listen, I'll be that party in her memory."

Crossing her arms before her, Maizie gave him a very penetrating look that all but declared she was *not* about to budge on this. "Now, you might as well talk to me because I'm not leaving until you do. If you plan on seeing any more patients today, you had better start talking, young man."

Chapter Fifteen

He wound up telling her everything.

It was against his better judgment, against anything he'd ever done, but he gave Maizie a condensed version of what had transpired, right up to Lily discovering the photograph of Irene and him, the one he had since thrown out.

Christopher secretly hoped that, in saying the words out loud, it would somehow help him purge himself of this awful deadness he was experiencing and *had* been experiencing ever since Lily had walked out.

It didn't. It just made it feel worse, if that was possible.

Desperate, he tried to describe to Maizie what he was feeling.

"It's like someone just sucked the very life force out of me." He shrugged, embarrassed. He was being weak and that just wasn't like him. "I'm sorry, I'm not explaining this very well and you didn't come here to hear me carry on like some twelve-year-old school-boy, lamenting about his first crush." He sighed, re-signed to his present state as he squatted down to the puppy's level to scratch the animal behind his ear. "I suppose you do remind me of my mother and I guess I just needed a sympathetic ear."

"Well, I'm very flattered to be compared to Fran-ces, Christopher," Maizie assured him. "Your mother was a very warm, wonderful lady." Touching his arm, she coaxed him back up to his feet. "You know what she'd say to you if she were here?"

He doubted that the woman had the inside track on his late mother's thoughts, but since he'd unburdened himself to Maizie, he did owe her the courtesy of lis-tening to what she had to say. Besides, he really did like the woman.

"What?"

"She'd ask you if you really cared about this Lily you just talked about and then, if your answer was yes, she'd tell you to not just stand there and grieve, but *do* something about it."

The laugh that Christopher blew out had no humor to it. "I think they call that stalking these days, Mrs. Connors."

In contrast, Maizie's laugh was light, airy and com-passionate. "I'm not talking about standing beneath this young woman's bedroom window, reciting lines from *Romeo and Juliet* or *Cyrano*. I'm suggesting doing something creative that would allow your two paths to cross—initially in public," she added for good measure.

Maybe the woman did have something up her sleeve.

At this point, he was willing to try anything. He felt he had nothing to lose and everything to gain.

"Go on," he urged.

"What does your young lady do for a living?" Maizie asked innocently as she stroked the Labrador. "Is she an accountant, or a lawyer, or—"

"She works for a catering company."

"A catering company," Maizie repeated, seeming very intrigued. "In what capacity?" she pressed, knowing very well that Lily was Theresa's pastry chef. "Cooking? Serving?"

"Lily bakes," he answered, although the word was hardly adequate to describe just what she could do. "Creating delicacies" was closer to the actual description, he thought.

Maizie made sure she appeared properly delighted. "Ah, perfect."

Christopher didn't understand. At his feet, the puppy who was Maizie's accomplice in this was beginning to chew the bottom of the exam table. Christopher took out a hard rubber bone and offered it to the teething puppy.

Walter took the bait.

"Perfect?" he asked Maizie.

"Yes, because I just thought of a plan. Every so often, the Bedford animal shelter has Adopt a Best Friend Day. The local businesses contribute donations or their time to help out."

Since he volunteered at the shelter, they had taken to sending him their newsletters. "I'm aware of those events, but I don't see—"

He never knew what hit him as Maizie went into automatic high gear. "I could pull a few strings, make a few suggestions, get this event up and running in, say, a week—two, tops—but probably a week."

How was this supposed to get Lily back into his life? "I still don't see how this has anything to do—"

Maizie held up a finger, about to make a crucial point. "Think how many more people might be attracted to come see the animals in the shelter if they knew that there were pastries being offered, the proceeds all going to keep the shelter operational? 'Come sample the pastries and go home with a best friend,'" Maizie said, coming up with a slogan right on the spot.

Then she eyed Christopher thoughtfully. "Didn't you say that you sometimes volunteer at the shelter, check out the animals, make sure they're healthy?" She knew the answer to that, as well.

His face lit up as his mind filled in the blanks, padding out what his mother's friend was telling him. "You know, that's just crazy enough to work," he agreed. "And Lily makes the most exquisite pastries." Christopher stopped short. He looked at her, slightly puzzled. "How did you know that?" he asked. "How did you know that Lily makes pastries?"

That had been a slip, but one that Maizie was quick to remedy. "I didn't. It was just a lucky guess," she told him. "I have a weakness for pastries."

"Well, if this gets her talking to me, Mrs. Connors, I'll make sure you get a pastry every day for the rest of your life," he promised, getting into the spirit of the thing.

"Which is guaranteed to be short if I start indulging like that," she told him with a laugh. Bending down, she picked up the puppy she had brought as a prop. "So, you're sure that Walter here is healthy?"

"Absolutely in top condition," he assured her. Christopher paused and regarded the Labrador thoughtfully as he scratched the dog's head. "He really does look like Lily's puppy," he told her.

"Then this Lily's puppy must be a very fine-looking dog," Maizie speculated with a wink.

She was quick to turn away and walk out before Christopher had a chance to see how broad her smile had become.

When she first heard about it, Lily's first inclination was to beg off. She knew that if she gave Theresa some excuse as to why she couldn't go to the catering event to serve her pastries, the woman would believe her and say it was all right.

But that would mean lying to someone who had been like a second mother to her. Not only that, it would be putting Theresa in a bind since she already found herself shorthanded. At the last minute, two of her regular servers, Theresa told her, had both come down with really bad colds, making them unable to work.

Lily didn't mind working, didn't mind being in the middle of things and hearing people rave about her desserts. But this particular event had to do with an adoption fair for the city's animal shelter. And that meant that Christopher might be there.

She knew that he volunteered his services at the shelter, that he periodically treated some of the animals that were left there. Funny how the very same thing that had made her love him now just made her feel uneasy.

It had been over two weeks since she'd walked out. Two weeks she'd been functioning—more or less—

without a heart. She hadn't taken any of his calls since that night.

The night that had been by turns one of the best and then worst nights of her life.

For a brief, shining moment, she had thought that she'd finally found the man she'd been looking for all her life. She and Christopher seemed to be of one mind when it came to so many things.

She had wound up running toward him when what she should have done was walked—slowly. Walked slowly and gotten to know the man.

But she hadn't, and then that bombshell had dropped, shattering her world.

Not only hadn't he told her that he'd been engaged, but he'd been the one to break off the engagement— and so recently. That meant he wasn't serious enough about his commitment. If he could break an engagement, walk out on a promise once, well, what was to keep him from doing it again? From bringing her up to the heights of joy only to let her fall onto the rocks of bitter disappointment somewhere down the line? Even if he could put all that behind him and change, that would take time for him to work out. He couldn't be ready for something so solid so soon after breaking off his engagement. He had to see that and once he did, he'd back away from her on his own.

She wasn't going to risk that, risk having her heart ripped out of her chest, risk tumbling down into the abyss of loneliness and despair. She just wasn't built like that. It was better not to dream than to have those dreams ripped up to pieces.

She hurt now, but she would hurt so much more later

if she continued seeing Christopher—continued loving him—only to be abandoned in the end.

"You are a lifesaver," Theresa was saying to her, the woman's very words of praise sabotaging any hope of remaining behind. "I am so shorthanded for this event, I might just have to put out a call to my children to have them come and help. This Adoption Fair promises to be huge." Theresa slanted a look at her protégée. "You are all right with doing this, aren't you, Lily?"

Lily forced a smile to her lips. There was no way she was going to let Theresa down—even if she spent the whole time there looking over her shoulder.

"I'm fine."

"This is for a good cause," Theresa said by way of a reminder. "But I don't have to tell you that. Once you take a pet into your home and into your heart, you see the other homeless animals in a completely different light. You outdid yourself, by the way." Theresa looked over to the boxed-up pastries that were all set to be transported. "Everything smells just heavenly, even through the boxes." Theresa beamed, then asked, "Are you ready?"

Lily snapped out of her mental wanderings. "You mean to go? Sure," she answered a bit too cheerfully.

She was ready to transport the pastries she'd made, ready to do her job. But as far as being ready to see Christopher again, the answer to that was a resounding no.

The best she could hope for was that he didn't show up. After all, it wasn't as if there were going to be any sick animals at the event. The object of this fair was to get as many of the shelter's residents adopted as possible. That guaranteed that only the healthy ones would be on display.

He probably wouldn't be there.

Lily was still telling herself that more than an hour later.

The adoption fair had gotten underway and it seemed as if at least a quarter of Bedford's citizens had turned out to check on the available animals and, as an afterthought, the food, as well.

Her pastries were going fast. She could only hope that some of the people doing all that eating were also seriously considering going home with one of the cats, dogs, rabbits, hamsters and various other species the shelter had on display.

"Your pastries are certainly a major attraction," Theresa said as she passed by the table where Lily was set up. "I think that by the end of the day, your 'contribution' will have raised the biggest amount of money for the animal shelter," Theresa told her with warm approval. In keeping with it being a charitable event, Theresa had charged only half her regular fee. "You should be very proud of yourself."

Although Lily did like receiving compliments, they always made her feel somewhat uncomfortable. She never knew what to say, how to respond, so she usually said nothing, only smiled. This time was no different. After smiling her thanks, Lily pretended to look off toward a group of children who were having fun with a litter of half Siamese, half Burmese kittens that had been born at the shelter. The mother, she'd been told, had been left at the shelter already pregnant.

Patting her hand, Theresa murmured something

about seeing how the others were doing and wove her way into the crowd.

No sooner had she left than Lily heard a voice behind her. "How much for that raspberry pastry?"

Lily stiffened. She would have recognized that voice anywhere. It was the voice that still infiltrated her dreams almost every night. The voice that made her ache and wake up close to tears almost every morning.

"Two dollars," she replied formally.

"Very reasonable." Christopher came around the table to face her. He handed her the two dollar bills and she pushed the paper plate with the aforementioned raspberry pastry toward him. Christopher raised his eyes to hers. "How much for five minutes of your time?"

"You haven't got that much money," she told him crisply.

More than anything, she wanted to flee the premises, to just take off and leave him far behind in her wake. But there was no one to cover for her and she couldn't let Theresa down after she'd agreed to be here.

She was just going to have to tough it out, she thought, hoping that she could.

"I've called you every day, Lily," he told her in a low voice so that they wouldn't be overheard. "You haven't returned any of my calls."

She looked at him sharply. Ignoring each call had been agony for her, especially the ones that came while she was home. The sound of his voice, leaving a message on her answering machine, would fill her house. Fill her head. He made it so hard for her to maintain her stand.

"I didn't see the point, Christopher. It wasn't going

to work anyway. Please just accept that," she told him as calmly as she could.

Now that he had her in front of him, he wasn't about to let this opportunity get away. "Lily, I'm sorry I didn't tell you about Irene, especially since it happened not too long ago. You have every right to be angry about that. I shouldn't have kept it from you."

"I'm not angry that you didn't tell me. I'm not denying that it didn't hurt, finding out that way, but that's not why I haven't returned your calls."

He looked at her, completely at a loss. "Then I don't understand," he confessed.

"*You're* the one who broke off the engagement. And how could you be ready to be with anyone yet?" she asked. "You made a commitment, Christopher. A *lifelong* commitment," she stressed. "And then you backed out of it just like that. Suddenly I come along, and who's to say you wouldn't drop me, just like that, too?" She snapped her fingers to underscore her point.

Unable to remain in the same space as Christopher any longer, she threw up her hands in despair and started to walk away. But she couldn't outpace him and she had a feeling that if she began to run, he'd only catch up. She didn't want to cause a scene, so she stopped moving. Maybe if she heard him out, *then* he'd go away.

"It wasn't 'just like that,'" Christopher contradicted, angry and frustrated by the accusation. "You didn't give me a chance to explain what happened. I wasn't just engaged to Irene for a day or a week, it was for five months—and during that time, she began to change from the person I thought I was going to marry to a completely different woman. Not only that, but she made it clear that she expected me to change as well, to transform into what she, and her family, felt was a suitable match for her and her world.

"I realized that our marriage wasn't going to be a happy one. What I'd pictured was going to be our life together just wasn't going to happen. She wanted me to give up being a veterinarian and go to work for her father's investment firm. In essence, she wanted me to give up being me and I couldn't do that.

"So I broke off the engagement, hired a moving company to pack up all my things and I came back to a place I always considered to be my home."

His eyes on hers, Christopher took her hand in his, in part to make a connection, in part to keep her from running off until he was finished. He still wasn't sure just what she was capable of doing in the heat of the moment.

"After the breakup, I was certain that the last thing I wanted was to be involved in another relationship, but I hadn't counted on meeting someone as special as you. You brought out all the good things I was trying so hard to bury," he confessed. "You made me feel useful and whole and you made me want to protect you, as well.

"I honestly didn't think I could feel this alive again, but I did and it was all because of you. I know how I feel about you." He tried to make her understand, to see what was in his soul—and to see how much she mattered to him. "I don't want to go back into the darkness, Lily. Please don't make me." His hands tightened ever so slightly on hers and he was relieved when she didn't pull them away. "I haven't been able to concentrate, to think straight since you walked out that morning. And frankly," he confided, his expression even more solemn than before, "the animals are beginning to notice that something's very off with me."

He made her laugh. Lily realized that it was the first time she had laughed since before she'd run out of his house.

"Let's just say—for the sake of argument," she qualified, "that I believe you—"

He jumped the gun and asked, "So you'll let me have a second chance?"

"If you did have a second chance at this relationship, what would you do with it?"

There was absolutely no hesitation, no momentary pause to think. He already knew what his answer would be. "I'd ask you to marry me."

She lifted her chin. He knew that meant she was preparing for a confrontation. "The way you asked Irene," she concluded.

"No, because I know now that the Irenes of this world are to be avoided if at all possible," he told her. "They don't want a husband, they want a do-it-yourself project. I want someone who loves me—who *likes* me for who I am and what I have to offer. More than that," he amended, looking into her eyes with a sincerity that almost made her ache inside, "I want you."

"For how long?" she challenged, even though she felt herself really weakening.

"I have no idea how long I have to live," he told Lily honestly, rather than resorting to fancy platitudes, "but for however long it is, I want to be able to open my eyes each morning and see you there beside me. These past two weeks without you have been pure hell and I will do anything, *anything*," Christopher stressed, "for a second chance."

"Anything?" she asked, cocking her head as she regarded him.

"Anything," he repeated with feeling.

"Well," she began philosophically, "you could start by kissing me."

He immediately swept her into his arms and cried, "Done!"

And it was.

Epilogue

"Well, ladies, I believe we can happily chalk up another successful venture," Maizie whispered to Theresa and Cecilia.

All three women were seated together in the third pew of St. Elizabeth Ann Seton Church. It was six months since the animal shelter adoption fair had taken place, resulting in more than one happy ending.

Maizie beamed with no small pride as she watched the young man standing up at the altar. He was facing the back of the church, anxiously waiting for the doors to open, and for the rest of his life to finally begin.

He looked very handsome in his tuxedo, Maizie couldn't help noticing.

Theresa dabbed at her eyes. No matter how many weddings she attended—and there had been many in the past few years—hearing the strains of "Here

Comes the Bride" never failed to cause tears to spring to her eyes.

"Frances should be here," Theresa told her two friends wistfully.

Cecilia leaned in so that both Theresa and Maizie could hear her. "What makes you think she isn't?" she asked in all seriousness.

Neither of her two friends offered a rebuttal to her question. The thought of their friend looking down on her son with approval as the ceremony unfolded was a comforting one.

"Oh, isn't she just spectacularly beautiful?" Theresa said in awe as they watched Lily slowly make her way down the aisle, each step bringing her closer to the man she was going to spend forever with.

"Every bride is beautiful," Maizie whispered to her friend.

"But some are just more beautiful than others," Theresa maintained stubbornly. Lily had become very special to her in the past year.

"Do you think she ever figured out how Jonathan just 'happened' to appear on her doorstep that morning?" Cecilia asked the others.

"I'm pretty sure she didn't. But I think that Chris might have a few suspicions about that," Maizie whispered back, thinking back to her impromptu visit to his office. He was, after all, a very intelligent young man.

"I told you that you should have used a different dog than one of Jolene's puppies," Cecilia reminded her.

Maizie shrugged. "Water under the bridge," she answered carelessly. "Besides," she went on with a grin her friends had always referred to as mischievous, "it did the trick, didn't it?"

"Shh, it's about to start." Theresa waved a silencing hand at her friends as she nodded toward the priest, who was standing at the front of the altar.

"Not yet," Maizie pointed out as she glanced over her shoulder to the rear of the church. Just before the doors closed, one more wedding participant had to make his way through the narrow opening.

A buzz went up in the church as guests nudged one another, each turning to look at the last member of the wedding party.

"Well, would you look at that."

"Certainly isn't your everyday member of a wedding, is it?"

"Aren't they afraid he's going to swallow the rings?"

The last comment had come from the man in the pew directly in front of the trio.

Unable to hold her tongue any longer, Maizie tapped him on the shoulder. When he turned around to look at her quizzically, she said, "They're not worried about the rings because that's the bride's dog and the groom did an excellent job training him. Besides, if you look very closely, both the rings are secured to that satin pillow in his mouth."

"Why would they include a dog in their wedding?" someone else asked.

The person's companion explained in a voice that said he was the final authority on the subject, "The way I hear it, if it hadn't been for that dog, the two of them would have never met and gotten together."

"Imagine that," Maizie murmured.

She slanted a glance toward Theresa and Cecilia, her eyes shining with amusement. What the young man had just said was the way Lily and Christopher might have viewed how their meeting had come about, but she, Theresa and Cecilia knew the whole story.

Maizie sat back in the pew, paying close attention to what was being said by the couple at the altar. She never tired of hearing vows being exchanged, sealing two people's commitment to one another.

This one, Frances, is for you, Maizie declared silently.

And then, just as with her two friends, her eyes began to tear.

* * * * *

Don't miss Marie Ferrarella's next romance,
COWBOY FOR HIRE,
available November 2014
from Harlequin American Romance!

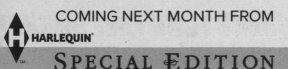

COMING NEXT MONTH FROM

HARLEQUIN®

SPECIAL EDITION

Available October 28, 2014

#2365 A WEAVER CHRISTMAS GIFT
Return to the Double C • by Allison Leigh

Jane Cohen can feel her biological clock ticking—she's ready to be a mom. For that, though, she needs Mr. Right, not the workaholic hunk she's fallen for! Casey Clay definitely isn't daddy material, she thinks. Especially since there might just be more to him than meets the eye, secrets that could change their relationship forever. Will Jane find her forever family with the man she has come to love?

#2366 THE MAVERICK'S THANKSGIVING BABY
Montana Mavericks: 20 Years in the Saddle! • by Brenda Harlen

When big-city attorney Maggie Roarke arrives in Rust Creek Falls, sparks fly between the beautiful blonde and handsome horse trainer Jesse Crawford. But one passionate night together has an unexpected consequence—namely, a baby on the way! Jesse is determined to wed Maggie and raise their child together, but a marriage of convenience might just turn out to be so much more.

#2367 THE SOLDIER'S HOLIDAY HOMECOMING
Return to Brighton Valley • by Judy Duarte

Sergeant Joe Wilcox is back where he never expected to be—Brighton Valley, which he left long ago. He's in town because he promised to deliver a letter for a fellow marine to Chloe Dawson, who broke his late pal's heart. But before he can do so, Joe is struck by a car and gets temporary amnesia. Joe can't remember who he is, but he's intrigued by the lovely Chloe. Can the soldier and his sweetheart find happily-ever-after just in time for Christmas?

#2368 A CELEBRATION CHRISTMAS
Celebrations, Inc. • by Nancy Robards Thompson

It's almost Christmas, but Dr. Cullen Dunlevy has his hands full. Recently named caretaker for his late best friend's children, Cullen needs help, so he hires the lovely Lily Palmer as a nanny. Lily believes wholeheartedly in the power of love and is determined to show her boss what it means to have holiday spirit. The dashing doctor might just have a family under his tree for Christmas!

#2369 SANTA'S PLAYBOOK
Jersey Boys • by Karen Templeton

Widowed high school football coach Ethan Noble is focused on keeping everything together for his four children. He doesn't have time to waste on love, even though his teenage daughter insists that her drama teacher, Claire Jacobs, would be the perfect stepmother. Claire's drawn to Coach Noble, but she thinks that the one show that's not right for her is their family saga. Will Claire come to realize that she could be the one woman to play the role of a lifetime—stepmom and wife?

#2370 DR. DADDY'S PERFECT CHRISTMAS
The St. Johns of Stonerock • by Jules Bennett

Dr. Eli St. John is forced to cut his bachelor lifestyle short to return to his hometown of Stonerock, Tennessee, and take care of his ailing father. While there, he does his best to avoid his ex, Nora, at all costs—after all, she was the only woman he ever really loved. To Eli's surprise, Nora's now a widow...and pregnant! Eli can't help himself from stepping up to help out, but time hasn't cooled the ardor between them. The doctor might be on the way to healing his own heart—and creating a family.

YOU CAN FIND MORE INFORMATION ON UPCOMING HARLEQUIN® TITLES, FREE EXCERPTS AND MORE AT WWW.HARLEQUIN.COM.

HSECNM1014

REQUEST YOUR FREE BOOKS!

2 FREE NOVELS PLUS 2 FREE GIFTS!

⟨H⟩HARLEQUIN®

SPECIAL EDITION

Life, Love & Family

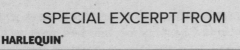
***

She exhaled noisily and collapsed on the other end of the couch. "Casey—"

"I just wanted to see you."

She slowly closed her mouth, absorbing that. Her fingers tightened around the glass. She could have offered him one. He'd been the one to introduce her to that particular winery in the first place. The first time she'd invited him to her place after they'd moved their relationship into the "benefits" category, he'd brought a bottle of wine.

She'd been wholly unnerved by it and told him they weren't dating—just mutually filling a need—and to save the empty romantic gestures.

He hadn't brought a bottle of wine ever again.

She shook off the memory.

He was here now, in her home, uninvited, and she'd be smart to remember that. "Why?"

He pushed off the couch and prowled around her living room. He'd always been intense. But she'd never really seen him *tense*. And she realized she was seeing it now.

She slowly sat forward and set her glass on the coffee table, watching him. "Casey, what's wrong?"

He shoved his fingers through his hair, not answering. Instead, he stopped in front of a photo collage on the wall above her narrow bookcase that Julia had given her last Christmas. "You going to go out with him again?"

Something ached inside her. "Probably," she admitted after a moment.

"He's a good guy," he muttered. "A little straightlaced, but otherwise okay."

She didn't know what was going on with him. But she suddenly felt like crying, and Jane wasn't a person who cried. "Casey."

"You could do worse." Then he gave her a tight smile and walked out of the living room into the kitchen. A second later, she heard the sound of her back door opening and closing.

He couldn't have left her more bewildered if he'd tried.

***

Find out what happens next in
New York Times *bestselling author Allison Leigh's*
A WEAVER CHRISTMAS GIFT, the latest in
THE RETURN TO THE DOUBLE C *miniseries.*

Available November 2014 from
Harlequin® Special Edition.

HARLEQUIN®

SPECIAL EDITION

Life, Love and Family

A Celebration Christmas

**Don't miss the latest in the
Celebrations Inc. miniseries,
by reader-favorite author**

Nancy Robards Thompson!

It's almost Christmas, but Dr. Cullen Dunlevy
has his hands full. Recently named caretaker for his
late best friend's children, Cullen needs help,
so he hires the lovely Lily Palmer as a nanny.
Lily believes wholeheartedly in the power of love
and is determined to show her boss what it means
to have holiday spirit. The dashing doctor might
just have a family under his tree for Christmas!

*Available November 2014
wherever books and ebooks are sold.*

HSE65850